Dax shifted, the dog alerting Hank that something was wrong.

Hank turned. The suspect had a gun. He lifted it, aiming at Hank's chest. That look in his eyes was one Hank had learned to spot before it meant it was too late. A crack rang out in the air.

Alena pivoted in the tiny cabin she'd been looking around. She stared at the open door. "Gunshot."

She raced to the door and jumped off the porch. She ran toward the sound, her heart pounding at what she might find.

Snow sprayed up and she spotted two men rolling on the ground. Tangled together, Hank fought with the suspect for the grip on his gun.

Alena spread her feet to stabilize her balance and yelled, "FBI! Drop the weapon or I will shoot you!"

Lisa Phillips is a British-born, tea-drinking, guitar-playing wife and mom of two. She and her husband lead worship together at their local church. Lisa pens high-stakes stories of mayhem and disaster where you can find made-for-each-other love that always ends in a happily-ever-after. She understands that faith is a work in progress more exciting than any story she can dream up. You can find out more about her books at authorlisaphillips.com.

Books by Lisa Phillips

Love Inspired Suspense

Colorado Manhunt
"Wilderness Chase"
Desert Rescue
Wilderness Hunt
Tracking Stolen Treasures

Secret Service Agents

Security Detail
Homefront Defenders
Yuletide Suspect
Witness in Hiding
Defense Breach
Murder Mix-Up

Visit the Author Profile page at LoveInspired.com for more titles.

TRACKING STOLEN TREASURES

LISA PHILLIPS

LOVE INSPIRED SUSPENSE
INSPIRATIONAL ROMANCE

LOVE INSPIRED SUSPENSE

INSPIRATIONAL ROMANCE

ISBN-13: 978-1-335-59924-7

Tracking Stolen Treasures

Copyright © 2023 by Two Dogs Publishing, LLC

Recycling programs for this product may not exist in your area.

For questions and comments about the quality of this book, please contact us at CustomerService@Harlequin.com.

Love Inspired
22 Adelaide St. West, 41st Floor
Toronto, Ontario M5H 4E3, Canada
www.LoveInspired.com

Printed in U.S.A.

Glory and honour are in his presence;
strength and gladness are in his place.
—*1 Chronicles* 16:27

To all the mistake makers, humans like me who don't always do the right thing but look to God for guidance. Keep walking the path He put in front of you. There is blessing ahead.

ONE

FBI special agent Alena Sanchez climbed out of the cab, dragging behind her the suitcase of things that weren't hers. She turned to the resort's main building, the location for this week's medical convention. Icy fingers ran down her spine that had nothing to do with who she was pretending to be.

This was about the chance to find a murderer.

She pulled her suitcase along the walkway. Her skirt swished around her knees and her heels clipped the cobblestones. A gust of winter wind whipped off the ski hills behind the resort buildings, peppered with skiers and snowboarders making their way back down off the snow for hot cocoa—and networking.

Alena fought the shiver. *I'm stronger than the fear.*

Local police were close if she needed backup. Security staff for the resort had been informed of her presence and her cover identity—just leaving out the fact she didn't have the targets' names. Yet. She'd worked undercover before, a handful of times. This was no different. They had a lead and she was here to follow it.

All she had to do was figure out if there was any credence to the tip they'd received.

As she approached the main doors for check-in, her cell phone rang. Alena dug it out of the designer purse she'd grabbed from the under-cover closet and saw her ASAC's name on the screen.

Why her boss's boss, Assistant Special Agent in Charge Brent Waterson, was calling, she had no idea. Maybe Supervisory Special Agent Torres didn't think she could do this, so she'd passed the issue up the ladder.

She refused to let go of the determination that drove her. The need she had deep inside to get the evidence, finally identify the suspect… and maybe even close the case. The way she believed God called her to do her job.

Alena slid her thumb across the screen. "Good morning, sir."

"Special Agent Sanchez, I trust you have a minute."

She pictured Brent Waterson in his office, straining his chair as he leaned back and stared at the ceiling the way he always did on the phone. Her boss was in the neighboring state, at the Cheyenne FBI office. Probably not much warmer than up here in Sundown Valley, Montana.

"I'm about to go in." Her stomach rolled as she stared at the doors ahead. *So close.* "Do I need to turn around?"

"No, stick with the assignment," Waterson said. "But I have an update for you."

Alena smiled to herself and headed in. "I'm at the check-in desk now."

The lobby was full of people milling around, suits and ties. It could be a room of FBI agents except for the fact the suits were designer and most men had a woman on their arm. The medical conference had been designed with couples in mind, having several events for the spouse of someone in the medical field. Couples seminars and workshops and a fancy gala tomorrow night.

Schmoozing wasn't why Alena was there.

She headed for the correct check-in line and shifted the phone away from her mouth to say, "Alena Sanders, hospital administrator."

The white-shirted volunteer leafed through a box of manila envelopes stuffed with information—and the lanyard everyone wore.

The ASAC said, "Listen up."

She kept her voice bland-sounding and said, "Yes?"

"The shooting victim we found three days ago has been identified. The ID came back as Brittany Hattenden. She's a pharmaceutical sales rep from Des Moines."

"That's great, Mom." She smiled at the volunteer and took the envelope. She mouthed *thank you*. An idea sprung into Alena's head. "I'm sorry, Mom. One second." She lowered the phone and asked the volunteer, "I wondered if my friend has checked in yet. Her name is Brittany Hattenden."

Waterson said, "Good thinking."

The volunteer nodded. "She checked in a few minutes ago. I remember because she had a little dog with her. So cute!"

"Thank you." Alena turned out of the line. She'd already checked into the hotel on her phone and had her room number. The resort app controlled entry to the spot where she was staying. She found a sign overhead and weaved between two doctors speaking a foreign language that sounded like Hindi. She'd never spent time on the Indian subcontinent, even though she'd lived overseas with her father at military bases all over the world. The general was retired now and lived with her in Cheyenne—as of a few months ago.

"If Brittany checked in for the conference, then whoever murdered her might've done it to take her place." She pushed out the lobby door and headed for her room. One in a block of chalets across a courtyard, each with a kitchen. Rooms that skiers preferred as it gave them easy access to the slopes.

Alena just wanted a place separate from the main resort hotel. She gripped the phone, now warm against her ear. "Whoever took the victim's place here has to be connected to the killer, and the whole case."

"It's a clear lead. You know what the victim looked like, and I'll send a copy of her ID. If she's got sense, this woman is close enough to resemble her if she wants to take her place. You watch your back." He paused. "I want regular updates." Waterson hung up.

These people had murdered someone a week ago. Three days earlier, a hiker had found the body. Now they knew why the young woman had been murdered.

Someone had wanted to take Brittany Hattenden's place and continue their scheme—scoping out the jewelry worn by the medical industry powerhouse couples at these events. Having fakes made, then, at the next opportunity, switching them out. The owners would have no idea they'd been duped. Until they had the item appraised.

Alena had a feeling this weekend was about

making the exchanges—stealing the real pieces and leaving behind forgeries.

All she needed to do was find a killer with an adorable dog. Not many guests would've checked in with a pet. That could help her narrow it down.

A woman wandered through the grassy area at the end of the parking lot. No snow had accumulated and Alena realized what was on the slopes had to be manmade to keep business going during a dry winter.

Alena let a van pass by, headed in the same direction as the woman. She crossed onto the cobblestone sidewalk on the other end of the parking lot. The adjacent chalet-style building had two floors. Alena's was at the end on the ground floor.

The van, probably here to make a delivery, headed toward the woman.

She got close enough to the end of the building to hear the woman over the van's engine.

"Come on, Kitty. Let's get out of the cold."

Alena couldn't make out her features from this far away, with the beanie she had on. The build and the long blond hair matched the dead woman's closely enough. This could be the person pretending to be Brittany Hattenden.

The van stopped at the curb. Alena set her suitcase by her front door and opened the app, her attention on the van while the driver got out and rounded the vehicle. Jeans, a dark jacket, a wool ski mask over his face.

The woman bent to scoop up her dog, unaware she was being approached.

"Look out!" Alena dropped her purse and started running in her direction.

She reached to her hip for her gun…the one she'd tucked in her purse—her only personal belonging aside from the phone. Her gaze searched the front of the van as she crossed the asphalt, headed toward it. No license plate. "Hey! Watch out!"

The dog started barking at Alena.

The masked man grabbed for the woman. She screamed, reeling back on her heels on the frozen grass.

"Stop!" Alena might believe this woman was a murderer, but she wasn't going to let her be kidnapped. Alena would lose her lead.

The man dragged her by the arm closer to the now-open door of the van.

Alena skidded on a patch of ice and started to slide. One leg buckled and her knee hit the ground. She cried out. The man grabbed the woman around the waist. The blonde screamed, launched her hands out and threw her dog at Alena.

Alena caught the dog on a reflex. It tried to

scramble out of her arms, so she grabbed the leash to make sure it at least didn't run off.

"Stop!" Alena tried to stand. Pain shot through her knee and she bit back another scream.

She gritted her teeth and pushed off the ground, ignoring the stinging in her knee. Inside the van now, "Brittany" screamed. The driver hit the gas and the tires squealed. They caught a patch of ice, but he righted the van and sped away.

The prime suspect in her investigation had just been kidnapped.

"So, do you wanna play basketball tomorrow or what?" SVPD officer Hank Miller sighed into the police K-9 vehicle. "Just call me back, Ev."

He tapped the dash screen and ended the call. Trying to catch his brother, Evan, was becoming harder and harder, but he'd arrived at the resort hotel now. That meant it was time for the team of officer and K-9 to get to work.

He knew the resort well enough. When he'd been in elementary school, his family had come here year after year. Until his parents bought a house on the slopes.

A year later, they'd been killed in a small plane crash on a return flight from a meeting his dad had in Denver.

Hank parked the car and sighed again. Someone had been kidnapped, and he was the Search and Rescue officer the community had insisted the chief hire. The fact he was a local played in his favor—especially when the rich folks who lived here learned his father had been Randall Miller. The other half of the residents of Sundown Valley respected his military service with the US Marine Corps. Kids in town wanted to know what it was like to sniff out IEDs. Not that it'd been Hank doing the sniffing.

Either way, he usually made headway with the locals while he was on shift as a cop.

The rest of the time, he preferred those slopes more than the populated streets in town. And the company of a certain four-legged boy getting excited in the back of the vehicle.

He thought through what he knew of the callout so far. The front desk had phoned in, saying one guest reported another guest had been kidnapped in a van. Given the crime rate in Sundown Valley—at least what was reported—the brazen nature of a daylight kidnapping was astounding.

But here he was.

With the back door up, Hank leaned in for the dog crate, anchored so it wouldn't slide around. Dax's tongue lolled out the side of his mouth.

The dog stood on all fours where he'd been asleep moments ago. "Hi, buddy."

Dax barked.

"Okay, let's go to work." Hank squeezed the latch on the crate and the door swung open.

Dax stayed where he was in the crate while Hank lifted the leash and reached in to connect it to the back of Dax's harness.

He took two steps back, the end of the leash in his hand. The K-9 didn't move. Right before the leash stretched taut, Hank stopped. Dax flinched but still didn't move, his whole body practically shaking to break the stay and hop out of the vehicle—and get to work.

"Yes." He said the word quick, sharp and high.

Dax launched from the crate and onto the ground beside Hank, where he skidded a fraction on the icy cobblestones but got his feet under him. He planted his doggy behind next to Hank's boot.

"Good boy." Hank clicked the button to lower the door and lock the car. "Let's go."

They walked together, Dax on his left side, keeping pace. He knew the dog preferred to run at any given time, so Hank only walked slowly when Dax needed to work out his self-discipline muscle. Considering he was barely two years old, that happened a lot. Dax would be a great dog in a year or so and was already pretty fantastic. Good thing Hank loved to run as well. They clocked a lot of miles on the trails around town.

Hank had served with K-9s for over five years between the Marines and the SVPD. He'd had a lot of dogs, but none stuck out as his favorite until Dax. This black Labrador retriever might be the dog of his heart, as some people called it.

The automatic doors to the hotel's main building slid open and the manager stepped between them.

"Hank, thanks for coming so quickly." The manager had black slacks, shiny black shoes and a white shirt over which he'd pulled a gray sweater-vest. Glasses hung from a chain around his neck and his gray hair had been trimmed recently. He stuck out his hand. "Nathanial Bremerton."

"No problem, Mr. Bremerton." Hank didn't know the guy, but most folks around town knew Hank and his brother. Those Miller boys who'd lost their parents and then driven their grandmother crazy. Shipped off to the military because the police chief had told them they were an inch from being arrested.

Six years later, they were both back in town, and had been for over a year. Making this work. Because what other choice did they have?

"This is the young woman who saw everything." The manager waved Hank to a sofa in front of the fireplace.

A tiny dog ran around the room, being chased by a woman in a black pantsuit.

Dax followed the chocolate-colored Chihuahua with each sniff from his nose and a well-trained eye for seeking whatever he'd been directed to find.

On the couch was a gorgeous woman with dark hair and a strong build, probably here for the medical conference. Her brow furrowed like she was deep in thought.

When he approached, she sucked in a breath and straightened, visibly pulling herself together. She spotted the vest on Dax. "Search and Rescue?"

"That's the plan." He motioned back to the door. Both he and Dax always preferred to search and then rescue—as opposed to the alternative of not finding the victim alive. "Can you accompany me outside?"

"Good idea." She stood, brushing her hands together.

Hank led the way to the door. "It's normal to be a little jittery after you witness something unsettling."

"I know." She nodded, striding with purpose beside him.

"I didn't catch your name."

"It's Alena."

"I'm Officer Miller. This is Dax." He motioned to his dog. "Just Alena?"

"For now. Because we need to find this woman." January wind whipped her hair around her face. "So, just Alena."

Hmm. "We" was pretty telling.

He didn't think she quite fit with this picture of an attendee at a medical conference. "What brought you to Sundown Valley this weekend? The conference?"

She stopped at the end of the parking lot between the main resort hotel and the ski chalets.

He overlooked the fact she hadn't answered why she was there and said, "Could you describe for me what happened?" She told him about a van and a young woman being dragged into it. As she spoke, he spotted a beanie on the ground. "Is that hers?"

Alena nodded. "It fell off her head."

"Any distinguishing features on the kidnapper? Hair color, skin color, tattoos or scars?"

She shook her head. "Just that ski mask over his face." She squinted, her gaze scanning the parking lot.

"What about the van?"

"No plate on the front. Then she threw that dog at me." Alena blew out a breath, amusement lighting her features for a second before it dropped away and she frowned. "Why would she *throw* her dog at me?"

Alena wasn't like any witness he normally met. "The Chihuahua from the lobby?"

Alena nodded. "A staff member agreed to watch the animal."

Dax shifted beside Hank's leg. He scratched the side of his dog's neck. "Soon, okay?"

Alena moved her weight from one leg to the other, antsy the same way Dax seemed to be. Maybe she needed a run, as well, some way to burn off restless energy. He was curious enough, Hank nearly asked her if she wanted to meet up later.

Except that would be a terrible idea. Not only was he on duty, but women tended to think such invitations were a date, and he had no interest in dating. After his ex-wife left him for another guy while he'd been deployed in Afghanistan, Hank had no reason to swim in those shark-infested waters again.

Not worth it.

"Thanks for telling me what you recall." He reached into his pocket for a business card so she could call him later if she remembered anything else. Alarm bells of intuition went off in his mind. Dax barked. The witness, Alena, spun around.

Hank needed to get her inside. Something was wrong. "We—"

The window of a car shattered. Twenty feet away. *Sniper.* Line of sight on the shot meant the intended target was them.

Another gunshot rang out across the parking lot. Hank grabbed her arm. "Get down!"

Someone was shooting at his witness.

TWO

"Stay here." The cop gave the order, his face close to hers.

Alena had to give him credit considering he'd acted quickly and saved her life. She watched him run toward the shooter, keeping to covered spots. His dog kept pace with him. It seemed like all three of them had noted instinctively the threat in the air.

There was something military about the way he moved—and that high and tight haircut. She should know, since her father was a marine corps general and she'd been raised in that life to rise to his exacting standards. Despite the fact he'd always told her how much she was like her mother, he'd wanted a tough kid, so he'd forged one in her.

What is going on here?

She spoke the question as a quiet prayer, mostly to focus her thoughts away from the existential ones that inevitably came when her life was on the line, and back to what was happening in front of her. She didn't need to tackle those big issues between her and General Sanchez when she'd just been shot at, her suspect had been kidnapped and there was a very nice-looking police officer chasing a suspect—or at least trying to find them.

She'd been shot at.

Hopefully, the cop would apprehend the shooter because she'd like to know who it was. And what on earth was happening here.

She watched him and his K-9 disappear into the trees, about to go to her room to call Waterson back and fill him in on what was happening, when a group of people ran from the lobby out into the parking lot and the courtyard area.

Fleeing because of the gunshots—they must have thought they'd be safer outside, not realizing that's where the trouble was. She waved them back. "Go inside, everyone! Wait until the officer says it's safe."

Right now she just wanted to solve this case, but the whole thing had unraveled in front of her. Now it just plain didn't make sense. Still, she should probably get out of the line of fire. Get her gun and her badge, and forget the whole undercover mission.

Alena couldn't see where the cop had gone, so she kept her head down and ran for the main doors. People were starting to come out. Curious about the commotion outside. She hadn't told the guy her occupation but could clear up the confusion soon enough—when she'd figured out what on earth was going on.

"Everyone, go back inside." She held up both hands and waved them toward the doors. "Please, take cover somewhere safe."

The shooting had stopped, but she didn't want an innocent person getting caught in any additional crossfire. She didn't need that on her conscience along with her colossal failure with Chadwell, her ex-boyfriend, a criminal only stringing her along as his girlfriend so he could get intel. The worst day of her career so far. When her personal life and her professional career had collided in a train wreck. She'd spent months clawing back the respect of her colleagues.

Alena spotted a woman—another guest— scoop up Brittany's dog and turn for the hall. The manager stepped in front of Alena. "Ma'am, I'm sure the police will be back in here soon. They'll take care of—"

"I'm the FBI agent you were told was coming." She didn't love cutting him off, but that woman was getting away. Alena needed the room number fake Brittany was staying in. "Thanks for your help with this."

Alena hurried down the hall and spotted the woman holding the Chihuahua, heading for the elevator. She caught up before the doors closed. "Hey, you got custody of the dog? What's your name?"

"Carol." The woman frowned. "Brittany is my roommate, and the staff lady said the dog is hungry, so I guess I get to feed her." Carol rolled her eyes.

Alena nodded, brushing back her hair like any other guest who'd had a stressful day. "I saw her get kidnapped. It was crazy. And then the gunshots? What is even going on?"

Maybe Alena should have a better opinion of corporate people, but she was waiting for one of them to prove her wrong. Being an FBI agent might've made her a little cynical, but having been raised by a man she'd decided was a stone-cold realist, it wasn't surprising she was the way she was. Military instincts. An investigator's mind.

She'd never had a boring job in her life, and would probably be terrible in the medical field with the need for patience and tact. She loved what she did.

So what kind of woman was this? And did she know what'd happened to fake Brittany?

Carol shivered. The dog peered at Alena from within what looked like a too-tight hold. "I can't believe this happened." She looked away to the side. "I only met her this morning, and now she's kidnapped? Am I next?" Carol sobbed.

Alena wasn't going to tell this woman she was an FBI agent if she could help it. Not when Carol could be lying. "I'm sure there's no need to worry. Unless there's a reason you think you might be a target." She tried to shiver the same way Carol had. "The police will find her, I'm positive."

If this woman had information, Alena needed it.

"I hope so." Carol shifted the dog in her arms. The elevator doors opened on four and Alena stepped out after her. She wasn't on this floor, but Carol didn't need to know that.

"How, I have no idea. I mean there's no way to know where that man took her." Alena paused like she was trying to puzzle it out. "Did she say anything to you about being scared something like this might happen?"

Carol shook her head. "We just met. I don't know if she was scared or not. She just went out for a walk on the trail before the first session tonight."

"Did she take her phone?"

"How should I know?" Carol flinched. "Actually she had her fitness tracker on."

That was good news. They could potentially

have a way to find Brittany. Did it have GPS on it? Maybe Waterson could get a warrant and find out. "If you let the police take a look at her things, they might be able to use that to find her."

The dog wriggled in her arms, so Carol let her down and held the leash while she sniffed around. Alena wondered how often the hotel had to clean up messes afterward.

The elevator doors slid open and the cop stepped out, his dog beside him. "There you are."

She took him in, black cargo pants and boots. A uniform shirt between the sides of his open heavy jacket. The name tag on his shirt said Miller and he had a red nose and ears from being outside in the cold with no hat.

"Find anything?"

Alena flinched, and not just about that very telling question. She didn't need to worry about him being cold outside. This was about her case, and despite the fact that she found him attractive, she had to focus. No thinking about him. No wondering if he might also find her attractive.

Bad ideas all around.

With her history in romance and the state of her career after that Chadwell disaster, she shouldn't even think about it for a second. Not even when Miller walked toward her and she got a look at the empathy on his face along with the breadth of his shoulders. And the lift of one eyebrow. "I did find something, actually."

Alena looked at his dog, just for the break from all that…man-ness. "Hi, doggy. Did you find the bad guy?" She didn't pet the black Lab and she wasn't about to ask if she could.

Miller cleared his throat. "We should find somewhere to sit."

"Because you need a statement?" He probably intended to see if something she said gave him a lead. Instead, Alena motioned to Carol. "This is Brittany's roommate, Carol. She says your vic was wearing her fitness tracker, and I was thinking maybe it can track her GPS. So, I hope that works out for you."

Alena turned to leave. Officer Miller snagged her arm, just enough to get her attention, and said, "My vic? I'm thinking I still need to talk to you."

She stared up at him. "I'm sure you do, but there's a missing woman to find. So how about you get that GPS info and go find her."

Alena could get the job done perfectly well on her own.

She didn't need a partner.

"I'm surprised you didn't say 'we.'" Out of the corner of Hank's eye, he spotted the roommate inching away from them. He motioned her back with a wave. "Ma'am, if you'd open the room door, please."

He already had the victim's phone, which he'd found on the ground close to where she'd been taken, tucked in his cargo pocket. Hank needed to find the victim, and the clock on that was ticking. But he also needed to figure out this woman in front of him.

Alena—no last name given—was the kind who could easily suck him in with her presence. Since there was a kidnapped woman to find, he wasn't going to let it affect him. It was just a reaction to a beautiful woman, after all. Not something lasting and real. Because he wouldn't allow it.

Hank and Alena followed Carol to the double doors of the suite at the end of the hall, Brittany's room.

Carol used her phone to unlock the door, the dog leash around her wrist now.

"That dog has diamonds on her collar I'd be more worried about losing than the animal." Alena's face flushed. "Maybe that's why she threw a Chihuahua at me."

"She wanted to save her beloved." Hank crouched for the collar. "Kitty? Apparently, that's her name." Then he grabbed his dog's face, running his hands through the K-9's ears. "Don't listen to any of them, you're better than diamonds."

Alena laughed. All trace of her reaction to being shot at—if she'd actually had a reaction in the first place—was gone now.

He turned to Carol. "If you and the dog would wait out here."

She said nothing. Hank let Dax off his leash. "Dax, find."

He didn't expect anyone to be in there, but he also didn't like surprises. Hank kept his hand on the butt of his gun, holstered on his belt, and stepped inside. Alena followed right behind, her shoes clicking the tiled entry to the hotel room.

He'd never even seen anyone who might've been a shooter outside. Now that he was back in here, and they had a lead—and the witness was unhurt, except for a limp she was hiding—he was retasking himself from an active shooter situation to finding Brittany.

Two officers he'd called over were outside and would continue to search for the shooter and talk to the hotel about looking at their security feeds. Even though he knew they claimed not to have any. Someone could have been killed, so if the resort had hidden cameras then the police needed to know.

Hank watched his dog search the room with his nose. "Who are you really?"

"FBI special agent Alena Sanchez." They both spoke in hushed tones so the roommate

wouldn't overhear, even though she was outside the room.

He glanced at her. "An FBI special agent?"
Hank got the impression she wasn't working
right now, or she'd have flashed a badge and
told him from the beginning. Maybe she was
here with a boyfriend—or husband. "Are you
here for business or pleasure, Special Agent—"

"It's still just Alena." Her expression gave
away nothing. "Did you see the shooter?"

He shook his head.

"Why kidnap her then shoot at us?" She
frowned. "All that would do is delay the response.
But they already got away with Brittany."

Hank thought on it while Dax disappeared
into the bathroom. "So they know you're here
and they're worried they'll be discovered."

"Which means Brittany is a victim, not the
suspect."

Dax reappeared before Hank could ask what
that meant. Either way, they were going to locate the missing woman. "He didn't find anything." Dax came back over, tail wagging.

"So why is he happy?"

The dog sat and Hank petted him. He wasn't
surprised she didn't know much about K-9s.
Most people never saw them work up close. "Because he's a good boy. Yes, you are. Good boy."
Hank pointed to the entryway. "Lie down."

Dax trotted away and slumped onto the floor with a groan, tongue hanging out.

Alena said, "Time to search?"

Hank looked at the room, pulling Brittany's phone from his pocket. The screen had shattered, but maybe their technician at the police department could get information from it. He called out, "Ma'am, could you come in and tell us which are her things?"

Carol entered, waiting until she was in the middle of the room before she set the dog down. Alena had used the word "suspect." But why would someone up to something criminal bring a tiny dog with them? Carol said, "Her things are over there."

Kitty scratched at a red suitcase in the corner. Alena crouched and flipped the lid. Carol watched as she pulled out an electronic tablet and a wallet. She tossed the dog two treats from a packet and came over.

Hank took the tablet, hoping it was connected to the fitness tracker. Thankfully there was no code on it—which probably meant it would turn out to be useless to their investigation. He found the app and pulled up the location. "She's not moving."

Alena said, "There's ID in here."

He spotted the cross streets on the map and used two fingers to zoom in on the dot. "I know where this is." He handed Carol his card then turned to Alena. "Let's go." On the way to the door, he said, "Dax."

They went back down to the elevator, Dax glued to his side. Alena took photos of the driver's license from the victim's purse. "Says Elizabeth Cunningham. The address is Colorado." She tapped on her phone. "Probably fake, but we'll run it and see what pops."

Hank frowned. "I thought her name was Brittany."

The doors slid open. "Come on."

This time he followed Alena out to the curb where he'd left his K-9 unit. "I have to get Dax situated, so get in." It would take fifteen minutes to get to the location of Brittany's fitness tracker, even with lights and sirens, and he also needed to call Dispatch to provide an update.

She climbed in his passenger seat without question.

Hank opened the crate and said, "Up."

Dax hopped in and turned around. Hank tossed him the jerky he always got to enjoy in the crate after he worked. They had a different reward for when Dax found whoever he'd been commanded to look for, but there hadn't been a search on this trip out of the car. Dax was still a good boy though.

Hank radioed the dispatcher that he was chasing the GPS location, which still hadn't moved, then he slid in behind the wheel. Later he could have Alena talk with his chief.

Hank headed for the spot from memory, to where that particular parking lot behind an old art gallery that had shut down backed up to the woods. Could be whoever had taken Brittany— or Elizabeth, if that was her name—knew the local area, but Hank couldn't know either way. He just hoped the guy hadn't killed her.

He pulled onto the blacktop and headed for town. "I'm thinking you should start talking, Special Agent Sanchez." He'd served under a guy with that name, but doubted the man was a relative of Alena's. Right now, there were more important things to discuss. "Why does the victim have two names?"

"At least you didn't order me to talk."

"Would that have worked?" He glanced at her, wondering how they got to bantering so fast. Some people it seemed just clicked into a rhythm, something he'd never had with his ex-wife. That meant he probably should've known it wasn't going to work out from the beginning, but he'd been a dumb twenty-one-year-old.

Alena chuckled. "Absolutely not."

Now that he was a far wiser thirty-one-year-old, Hank could honestly say he knew better. Steer clear of love and he'd keep his heart intact. That was how he planned to leave it with Alena, even if she was gorgeous. It wasn't like she'd stick around anyway.

"So where are you from?"

"I work out of the Cheyenne office in Wyoming."

"Major crimes?"

"White collar, mostly." She paused.

Waiting to see how he would react to that? Like he'd think less of her because she didn't solve gruesome murders? Maybe that said more about how she viewed herself than whatever weight his opinion might carry.

"Okay," he said just to encourage her to continue.

"There's a small group, possibly only one or two people. We've been tracking them through the latter part of last year, trying to get a lead on who they are, watching them travel across the country to resorts exactly like the one Brittany is staying at. Medical or investing conventions mostly. People with high incomes who collect in groups."

"And your role in this is…?"

She said, "The supervisory special agent in my office believes they'll head to Spokane next, but I've been watching their movements. Tracking them. Sure, we all have. Everyone on the team wants to find them. But I was handed an anonymous tip they'd hit this place next. They killed the real Brittany days ago. Elizabeth Cunningham—if that's not a fake ID, too—took Brittany's place here."

"What does this crew do?"

"They scope out a group and catalog jewelry. Necklaces, bracelets and rings. They have fakes crafted—good ones, too. They switch them out so the vic doesn't know their stuff was stolen until the thieves are long gone."

Hank had no idea about sophisticated white-collar crimes. He'd never worked any cases like that. "How does that work? People don't know their stuff went missing?" Seemed to him like a lot of fuss just for a payday.

"They scout out jewels at events," Alena said. "Take pictures like it's just shots of the evening and everyone they're around partying with, to show off for social media. Things like that. Then they have someone create forgeries and find a time to sneak into the person's room and switch the necklace, or bracelet, out for a quality forgery." She sighed. "We think they do multiple switches at one event, so it's one big payday. These people collect at conferences and symposiums like it's their high school reunion, catching up with each other."

Hank made a right turn, minutes from where

the dot had been. "How does the victim know their stuff is fake?"

She shifted in the seat and he wondered if she was sore from hitting the ground to avoid being shot. Other than that, she seemed to be completely unfazed. Considering she was an agent, it wasn't surprising, even if she worked highbrow crimes that might be far less violent.

Alena said, "They take it in to be appraised, or to sell, and they get bad news about the real value. Most don't want to admit they've been duped. But they still want to claim the insurance payout, so they have to open a case with law enforcement to satisfy the underwriters."

"Huh."

"And you work Search and Rescue?"

"I'm just a beat cop. Dax is the one who does the real work." She glanced at him, but thankfully, they were already there. "The location hasn't changed, right?"

She woke up the tablet, then put her thin gloves back on. "Doesn't look like it. Still right here."

He drove around the empty closed-down building, past the overflowing trash bins, to the lot behind it. Not the nicest part of town. One the visitors to the resort and other tourists who brought the winter season alive tended to steer clear of.

A van came into view.

Alena gasped. "That's the same vehicle. The one she was tossed into."

He slid out his gun. Dax would be fine in the vehicle for a few minutes, long enough to check things out. "Are you here officially?"

Alena bent down and slid a backup weapon from her boot. "I don't have my badge on me. Just so you're aware."

"All right. Let's go." He led the way to the van, gun up as he checked around. Then in the windows. He stood to the side while Alena pulled the handle to the door on the side.

It slid open.

"Empty." Hank blew out a breath.

She lifted the fitness tracker from the floor with a gloved hand. "So, where is she?"

He backed up and rounded the front of the van, looking at footprints on the ground. "I'll get Dax." Hank's gaze followed the prints to the tree line. "Looks like they're on foot."

THREE

"You really think he parked right here just to drag her through the woods?" Alena followed behind Officer Miller and his dog. She'd decided to think of him as Miller, not Hank, to maintain that professionalism between her and the cop. Especially now that he knew she was an FBI agent.

Much better than thinking of him as a man, all strong and tall and... *Enough.* She heard her father's voice in her head.

For good or ill, all those things General Sanchez had drilled into her had stuck around. Her dad had hardwired her to be able to focus, to operate at peak physical fitness and to push to win at everything. She hadn't spoken to her father about her love life since her ex-boyfriend Chadwell had revealed himself to be part of an art forgery ring and she'd had to put cuffs on him and drag him to the FBI office in Cheyenne.

Dating her just to get close to an FBI agent so he could continue to get away with his crimes.

"I think Dax will figure it out either way."

Alena blinked and her thoughts whipped out of the past back to the present. Right, Brittany and her kidnapper in these woods—and a Search and Rescue K-9 on the case. She needed to let Chadwell, and his betrayal, go. That wasn't part of her life anymore, even if she acted like it had happened just yesterday.

She sighed, long and loud.

"Doing okay back there?" Hank called over his shoulder from up ahead, his dog out in front of him following the scent.

"Yeah. I'm good." Did he think she was having a hard time hiking this ascent? Maybe she was giving that impression, but it wasn't like she would be explaining all her issues to this stranger anytime soon.

"So who is the vic, anyway?" Hank asked. "And what do you think her involvement is?"

"She's one of them. Connected somehow." After all, she was pretending to be a murdered woman, someone who would have had access to this convention. Alena had presumed earlier that was why she'd been killed—to gain entry to this event with her ID. She still figured the dead woman was a means to an end, whether or not she was a member of the crew or an accomplice.

"But you haven't identified them yet?"

She had no idea if the kidnapper was part of the crew as well. But why turn on an associate like he had? "Three of them, maybe four. We know that much."

"But the roommate is clean? Carol, whatever her last name was?"

"We'll check her out, as well, but right now Brittany is the priority."

"Agreed."

The trail from the lot couldn't be wider than what deer had tracked out coming off the mountain for food. The question was whether this had been planned. A premeditated kidnapping that would lead to murder. It certainly hadn't felt like a spur-of-the-moment snatch of a victim. Nothing about this was ordinary.

Had the kidnapper planned this route? "I don't see how anyone could've hauled Brittany up here without breaking some branches. Did she walk?"

Hank slowed and reached out a hand. "Broken like this?" His grip snagged a branch on the move then let it go so it pinged back into position.

A broken branch didn't mean Brittany was unconscious and it also didn't indicate she was ambulatory either. She could be dead, but there hadn't been any blood in the van or on the trail on the way up. Right now, they had no idea what condition she was in.

Hank's voice drifted over his shoulder again. "You feel like telling me why someone might've been shooting at you earlier?"

"You didn't find the guy, right?"

Dax slowed on the trail, sniffing as he moved left instead of continuing forward.

Hank glanced at her. "I never saw a shooter, or even where he might've shot from. If it was a 'he.' So how about you answer the question? Is it related to the case or is it related to you?"

Alena hissed out a breath between her teeth. "He could've been aiming at you, for all we know. Anyone in your life who wants to kill you?"

Dax caught the scent again and started forward. They both followed, walking closer now, almost side by side.

Hank sighed. "So, assuming no one knows you're here except the FBI, the man who took our vic is unlikely to have doubled back just to shoot the witness."

"A partner, then." Alena could see how that made sense. "There are three or four of them. But why would one do this? Unless it's a rival or a personal issue she has."

"Or the two events are completely unrelated,"

Miller said. "Tell me about the case you're working and why you think Brittany is involved."

Alena said, "The murder victim or the kidnap victim?"

"Both, I guess."

"It boils down to the fact someone with the name Brittany Hattenden was on location every time an item was switched out." Alena scanned the trees on the hill to her left and then the overhang developing on the right where the ridge dropped off to nothing as the trail turned and they wound upward parallel to the town below.

She continued, "So far, we've gathered about half a dozen items that have been switched out. Single items show up on the black market for sale, so maybe they hold on to them, waiting for the right time to offload them so it's not as noticeable as flooding the market."

"But no IDs?" He glanced over at her, but mostly watched his dog search.

She had to admit, it was cool to see a K-9 in action. She'd never had a dog but had always wanted one. "From hotel surveillance the night of one of the thefts, we know at least one man and one woman are involved, but we don't have an image of their faces. Just their body shape and height. That kind of thing. Brittany fits the ID we've got so far, but so do a lot of women."

This whole thing had suddenly become very

complicated. Alena didn't need three cases to work this weekend, even if the kidnapping was technically Officer Miller's. She couldn't investigate a shooting where she was the target. And that was fine. As far as she was concerned, she would work her case.

"Dax has something."

She leaned around the officer to look. The dog eased to the edge of the trail, where it dropped off to the street below. He sat.

"Good boy." Hank patted him on the head then peered over the edge. He grabbed his radio. "This is K-9 One."

Alena moved to the rim of the trail and looked down.

He gave the closed-down store address. "Requesting an ambulance at this location."

She winced. Brittany lay sprawled on the grass about fifteen feet below, rolled so she was almost facedown. But she looked unconscious. "I think I can get to her."

Miller grasped her elbow. "Let's wait. The EMTs might need the fire department and their equipment to help get her back up here."

"That will take time she might not have." Alena spied Brittany's head. "She's bleeding, which means she's still alive. The clock is running."

She traced a viable route with her gaze then

grabbed the trunk of a sapling that fit in her hand. Her fingers curled around it and tested how much give the young tree had before she moved.

Alena picked her way down the steep hill.

With Dax tucked away asleep in the car, Hank strode through the automatic doors of the emergency room. Alena walked beside him. She'd been quiet on the way to the hospital, probably exhausted from the day and everything that'd happened to her.

She'd descended the hill and assessed Brittany, and he'd waited for the EMTs. Dispatch had sent the firefighters who worked Rescue, and two were certified medics. They'd rappelled the hill, loaded Brittany into a basket and brought Alena back up with them. Each man of the four-person team had fawned over Alena and her bravery at going down there, chatting with her as they all walked back to the lot behind the closed store.

Leaving Hank to bring up the rear with Dax, not talking to anyone.

She hadn't been entirely comfortable with the attention, but Alena seemed like the kind of woman used to conversing with a group of guys. In a way that made him think maybe she'd been a tomboy in high school.

She was probably as tired as Dax, who had quickly lapsed into a satisfied slumber the minute he'd hit the padded bed in his crate.

Hank would've preferred this FBI agent be as easy to figure out as his K-9 partner. Then again, he'd been with Dax over a year now. Alena he'd met only hours ago—and he was intrigued, to say the least. Still, that wasn't the point. He was more interested in this case and who had tried to kill her.

Assuming it hadn't been a local shooter aiming at *him*.

"Hank!" The desk attendant smiled widely and tipped her head to the side so her hair fell over her shoulder. "Dax is a hero again, or so I hear."

"That he is."

The FBI agent stopped beside him. "We'd like to speak with Ms. Hattenden." Alena looked down at the attendant's ID badge. "If that's okay, Wanda." She gave the woman a polite smile.

Wanda lifted the phone on the desk. "Let me check if she woke up yet."

"Thank you." Alena turned and put her back to the counter. She surveyed the waiting area, the bustle of the entrance to the ER and the bays where patients were being treated. It was a huge circular room with a low ceiling but plenty of alcoves and places for people to wait.

Hank just surveyed her. As he watched, she suppressed a shudder. Too many people. Too enclosed? She might be more shaken up by the day than she wanted to admit. He said, "You doing okay?"

"Sure, why wouldn't I be?"

He wasn't convinced. "So you're the type to shove it all down and go on like everything's fine?"

"Isn't that the way you military guys do it?"

He frowned. "How'd you know?" He wore long sleeves, so it wasn't like she could see the tattoo of his unit on his arm.

She shrugged. "I just know." She eyed him. "Marine corps, right?"

"Is that a bad thing?" Hank frowned. "Because you have something against marines?"

Wanda frowned, listening on the phone but apparently also listening to his and Alena's conversation.

"Hardly." Alena snorted. "I was raised by one."

"Hold up," Hank said. "Sanchez. As in General Manuel Sanchez?"

Alena nodded. "He's retired now, but yeah. He's always been that guy, even back when he was a drill sergeant."

"I know what you mean." Hank felt his grin spread wide. "He visited us in Kabul. Spent one morning doing PT with my squad." He chuckled. "Challenged one of my buddies to a push-ups contest."

"Of course he did." The edge of a smile graced her lips, but it quickly bled away.

"Are you sure you're all right?"

"Long day." Alena blew out a breath and lifted her chin at someone. "And it's not over yet."

He turned as a nurse approached them.

"She's awake, and you can have ten minutes." The nurse was older. She glanced between them. "Given everything she's been through, she doesn't need to be hounded by the police."

Alena said nothing, so Hank nodded. "No problem. Thank you."

The nurse spun away. "Follow me."

Alena glanced at him. He caught the look on her face but didn't get the chance to comment on the nurse's statement, or her assumption they were there to "hound" Brittany. He wasn't, at least. What he wanted to know was what Brittany had been through, and what she'd told the nurse. Given patient confidentiality, they needed Brittany to tell them what happened. But if she was tangled up in a criminal lifestyle, would she reveal the truth?

The nurse pulled the curtain back. Brittany's face immediately started to crumple at the sight of the staffer. She was lying under a pile of blankets and apparently the nurse was a reason to sniffle and be upset. Then she saw Alena and Hank, sniffed, and composed herself for their sake. A woman who played the crowd like a pro.

The difference between the two reactions was stark. First Brittany crumpled for a medical staffer she might need sympathy—or meds—from. Then for two cops who had the authority to arrest her, Brittany closed off her expression.

He took the lead with the witness since he was in uniform and Alena didn't have her badge out. "I'm Officer Miller with the K-9 Search and Rescue Unit. This is—"

Alena cut him off. "We're the ones who found you on the mountain." She gave the victim a polite smile. "Do you remember us?"

Brittany stared at Alena. Hank couldn't help wondering if Alena was testing the young woman, seeing what she knew or if she would be open with them. Brittany said, "Should I?" She made a face. "You were at the resort. Where's Kitty?" She pushed off the blankets and sat up. "What did you do with her?"

The nurse whipped the curtain open.

"She took my dog!"

After a scathing glance at Alena, the nurse tucked her back in. "You need to lie down, dear. You need to get warm."

Brittany lay back, sniffed and nodded.

Alena rolled her eyes. Hank had to scratch his chin to hide the smile behind his hand. Alena said, "Ms. Hattenden, you *threw* your dog at me."

"She's precious!"

"She's with your roommate, Carol." Hank tried to appease her. "I'm sure they're both fine."

"Well, I'm not!"

She didn't indicate anything about the roommate, but Hank wouldn't be convinced she wasn't possibly part of this until they proved it otherwise.

Alena pressed her lips together. Hank figured he'd continue the questioning, whether she responded better to him or not. "Ms. Hattenden, do you know who abducted—"

"Bring me my dog!" Brittany's face reddened. "I need her!"

Hank wasn't going to argue about the hygiene of having a dog in a hospital. "Can you identify the man who took you?"

"He wore a mask." She bit off the words, tears in her eyes.

He kept his voice soft and asked, "Can you tell us what happened?"

"I was kidnapped." Brittany untucked a hand to wave it at Alena. "She should know. She was there." The young woman sneered. "She was probably in on it."

Hank turned to Alena, raising his eyebrows so she'd get the idea she should tell Brittany she was an FBI agent, not in collusion with a kidnapper.

"Brittany," Alena said, "you were kidnapped in broad daylight right in front of me, driven across town and dragged up a hill."

"He pushed me over! He was going to kill me!"

"And yet you sustained only scratches. So whatever his plan was, he didn't succeed." Alena moved closer to the end of the bed. "Seems a little convenient, if you ask me." The last part was said under her breath, so only Hank caught it. Then she said, "That means you're stronger than him, Brittany. You got away."

Brittany started to bluster.

"That's a good thing." Alena stepped closer to her. "You survived."

Hank caught the edge of something in her tone that made him want to ask her about her story. They might get there before she left town, and they might not. But he knew he was curious about her.

Alena said, "After you were taken away in that van, someone shot at us. Do you know who?"

"How would I? I was kidnapped!" Tears fell down her cheeks.

Hank didn't know whether to put the pressure on or find some empathy. "Can you walk us through what happened?" He'd rather have asked for her to confirm her real ID, or run her prints. Brittany had to believe they thought she was the victim here, and nothing else. Not that the FBI suspected she was part of the crew.

"I've already told you. I was kidnapped!"

The nurse whipped the curtain back but didn't step in. "Time for both of you to leave. Your ten minutes is up."

"We will be back to talk to you soon," Alena told Brittany.

Hank pulled out his business card. "If you think of anything at all that might help us find him, please call me. Thanks for speaking with us." He closed the curtain himself.

Alena had already walked out ahead of him. Hank jogged through the ER to catch up to her.

"Hey."

She glanced over her shoulder at him but said nothing.

"You think that whole thing was a setup?"

She might have Brittany on her radar as a suspect on her FBI forgeries case, but that didn't mean this hadn't been a real kidnapping.

They walked all the way to his car before Alena said, "I needed to see how she would react to being pushed a little. A lot of that was bluster, or drama, but I don't know if it was for our benefit or the staff." She pulled the door open. "She has to know we're onto her now—or at least suspect it, since she's on our radar and we didn't treat her like any other victim."

Hank jogged around and climbed in, turning to look in the back. In the dome light overhead he spotted Dax barely open one eye. "Hey, buddy." Hank flipped the light back off. He pulled out of the hospital parking lot. "The resort?"

It was getting dark now. Dax would be looking for dinner, and Hank would need to let him be a dog instead of the cop the department needed him to be whenever they called. Not that Dax cared. He liked to work, and he liked to be lazy just as much. He had a very balanced approach to life.

Alena bringing up her father earlier made him wonder about his brother and the fact Evan hadn't called him back. The guy was the only family Hank had left since their grandma died three years after their parents' deaths. At least Alena still had her father. General Sanchez put out a newsletter each month for veterans. Hank read it as soon as it showed up in his inbox. He'd never once wavered in his opinion of the old man.

Why did it seem Alena wasn't all that en-
thuscd about hcr dad?

"Yeah, if you could take me back to the resort, that would be great." Alena nodded. "I
don't have anywhere else to be."

"How about we reconvene tomorrow?" he
suggested. "It's my day off, but Dax and I can
put in some overtime. Get the reports done. Talk
to Brittany some more, see if she remembers
what happened." Or the possible identity of who
had taken her. "Follow up with hospital staff and
the other officers who responded."

"Sure." Alena checked her pockets and pulled
out her phone. "I want to talk to Brittany again,
and she seemed to take a shine to you."

Hank wasn't going to touch that comment.
"Great. I'll let the front desk know when I arrive in the morning."

Alena waved him around the side of the main
building, to a long building. Rows of ski chalets
definitely in the midrange nightly rate. "One
from the end. Sixteen. You can just knock after
breakfast."

"Seven?"

She chuckled. "I meant after normal people
breakfast, not marine corps breakfast, but if you
bring me coffee, you've got yourself a deal."

Hank pulled into a space outside the room
and immediately noticed a vertical strip of black

between her door and the frame. "I'm guessing you didn't leave that open."

"No, I did not." She pulled her gun again.

Hank got out as well. "Let me." This was his jurisdiction. He eased the door open but heard nothing, then he reached in and flipped the light on. "Oh, boy."

A breath escaped Alena's lips in a rush. "Everything…"

Her belongings lay strewn across the floor, the bed, every surface. The sheets had been shredded, as though someone with a knife slashed them to strips. They'd opened her suitcase and tossed her things all over.

Hank's jaw tightened. "Someone is out to get you."

FOUR

Alena stared at the room. She hadn't even un-packed, and now everything she'd brought lay across the bed and the floor. Pulled out and tossed around. It didn't look damaged, at least. Neither did it look like whoever had done this had been searching for something.

She had no idea what their motives were. Bottom line, they'd taken everything she had here and strewn it all over.

She bit the inside of her lip. *You don't scare me.*

Cold rolled over her with the night breeze and she shivered. The last time she'd let the fear get to her… She couldn't think about that, or the fact her ex, Chadwell, hadn't ended up in prison. Despite his clear guilt, he was still on the streets.

Her faith had died with his charges. The day he'd walked out of a cell, back on the streets, she'd given up hanging on to trust that wasn't working.

God didn't listen to her.

Alena slid her phone from her pocket. "I need to call my ASAC."

She started to step into the room, out of the cold, but Hank stayed her with a hand on her arm. "Hang on, okay? Let's do this right. Want to sit in the car?"

She ended up walking that way with him, and Hank got on his radio. He called in the break-in. Asked for officers to bring evidence collection kits.

Once again, she was the victim. *Hardly.* She might've been shot at, and now her privacy violated in this way, but that didn't make her the target. "This might've been someone trying to figure out who I am, and whether I'm a threat."

"Was anything taken?"

"Not that I saw. I didn't pack much that was personal."

Hank glanced over. "One of the officers will bring the manager over. I'll stay here with you."

"I don't need to be babysat. I can work a scene."

"You can also let us do this, since it's Sundown Valley PD jurisdiction until we know for sure this connects to your federal case."

Alena frowned. So he was a by-the-book kind

of guy? Good. Too many cops let things slip, which was precisely the reason Chadwell had walked—because his lawyer had argued a technicality that looked like a violation of his human rights. Maybe his right to continue breaking the law.

"You okay?"

"Why does it seem like you keep asking me that?" She shook her head. "I'm fine. Most of that isn't even my stuff. I'm supposed to be undercover, so it's not like I brought a lot of personal effects. Just some clothes—which can be replaced."

"Okay, then."

"Maybe you should worry more about finding whoever did this than making sure I'm 'okay.'"

The corner of his lips curled up. Dax shifted in the back and Alena felt a puff of his warm breath.

She ignored the obvious icebreaker and said, "Maybe Dax can sniff them out."

"Oh, he will." Hank's mouth spread into a smile.

"This isn't funny."

His smile fell. "No, it isn't. But it seems I have a type."

Alena shifted under the intensity of his gaze. "What does that mean?"

"I'll tell you later. Right now, there's work to do." He pushed open his door.

She got out, as well, and heard Dax let out a little whine. The K-9 probably wanted to be in the center of the action—she felt the same. Just because it was her hotel room didn't mean she would be sidelined.

If it wasn't so late, she would head over to Brittany's room and speak to Carol. Find out what seemed off about the woman. Ask if she'd ever met Brittany before today, and how they'd come to be roommates.

This conference was supposed to be about networking for people in the medical field. Whatever the crew of thieves was up to, Alena had apparently ventured too close to figuring it out. It seemed like she'd barely scratched the surface showing up here and suddenly she was being shot at? Someone wanted to know who she was.

Thankfully, she hadn't left her badge in that room, or they'd have discovered her status as an FBI agent right away.

"So you're the fed?"

She spun to find an older uniformed officer with chevrons on his jacket sleeves, and stuck her hand out. "Sergeant. I'm Special Agent Sanchez."

"Jaker. Nice to meet you." He headed for her room. "Let me know if anything was taken."

She followed the sergeant while Hank stood with another officer talking to the resort manager. She'd been so deep in thought she hadn't even noticed them come over, and now wasn't the time to be distracted.

Alena stepped into the room after the sergeant and looked at the mess.

"How'd you leave it?"

"Not like this." Alena winced. "I hadn't even unpacked. The suitcase was by the door, because I didn't even have time to come in here with the kidnapping and the shooting. I just rolled it in and locked up."

He nodded. "Anything stolen?"

Alena walked through the room. The carpet was older, and her things needed to be put away before anyone else saw. Except the cops would see everything before that happened. It was part of the job, so she shouldn't be embarrassed. Cops saw a lot worse than her personal items.

She sighed. "It was just clothes. I have my phone for notes and contacting my ASAC. Which I need to do."

She couldn't help feeling like she was in over her head. Maybe that was just looking at her room, seeing the destruction, and feeling the itchy sensation of knowing someone had touched her things.

"Any idea why you're suddenly a target?"

Alena chewed her lip for a second. "Only theories. That Brittany might've been kidnapped as a warning. Like maybe she was getting cold feet, so she was taken as a threat to remind her she isn't in charge. Whoever she works for won't let her out of their bargain."

"Evidence?"

"I'm hoping I can talk to her. Get her to tell me who she's working with. Or for." Often the FBI made an agreement with a witness up to their neck in something. If the person felt like they had no choice, cooperating was their way out. So the FBI wired them up—electronically, which meant wirelessly—and sent them in to get their boss, or partner, to confess.

"If she got kidnapped, she's not the top of the food chain."

"Yep." Alena headed for the door, not wanting to look at her clothes anymore. Her phone buzzed in her hand, but it wasn't her ASAC calling. It was her dad. She would have to call him back in a second.

Hank came over when she stepped out. "The manager can get you a new room, if you'd like that."

Alena had an idea. "How about one on the same floor as Brittany?"

"You're going to keep working this case?"

"It's a weekend conference. By the end of it, I'll have evidence to make an arrest, or I won't." Having a time limit gave her the ability to push aside the fear. And that icky feeling of someone being in her room, touching all her things.

Alena would rather be out, working the case—which meant she needed a rental car so she could do that.

She didn't think this break-in was about something creepy. This wasn't personal when it had likely been a fact-finding mission. Someone looking for information about who she was. Though, they could've done that without making a mess. Had they cared to keep it a secret that they'd been in her room.

Whoever did this had to suspect she was a cop.

There had now been ample opportunities to discover who she was if someone was watching her. She'd interviewed Brittany—or rather, Elizabeth Cunningham, if that was her name— after all, and acted like a law enforcement officer. An astute observer would have put two and two together.

Nothing about any of this made sense—least of all the timing of a shooting where Alena was the target, and this break-in.

Considering they hadn't tried to hide their presence in her room, they didn't care if she knew—which meant they didn't consider her a threat to them.

Whoever it was, they were going to discover that Special Agent Alena Sanchez was a very real threat to their walking free to continue breaking the law.

She just had to figure out who they were.

Hank watched her head for the resort manager, that confident FBI stride back in place. At first when they'd realized her room had been broken into, she'd been knocked back a step. A blow to her privacy, as well as her work here and the authority she had.

Alena Sanchez was an FBI agent, but she was also a woman. Anyone was vulnerable, male or female, but some people seemed to think women were an easier target.

Hank was going to find whoever had done this and explain they were wrong about that.

He didn't like that Alena's first trip to Sundown Valley had resulted in both a shooting and a break-in only hours after her arrival. She might be here to work, but he wanted to show her the good parts of town. Take her to the diner on Main Street and get her a slice of apricot pie, his mom's favorite.

Hank needed to focus, so he headed for their huddle in time to see the manager start to bluster.

"You have to understand, Special Agent Sanchez," the older man said. "This resort hotel takes the privacy of our guests with utmost seriousness."

"You're telling me you have no security cameras." Alena folded her arms.

He saw in her stance a reflection of her father's mannerisms. General Sanchez was basically a hero of his. Hank had seriously undersold that. He'd taken to sitting with his phone out, email open, waiting for the monthly newsletter the day the general sent it. Lately, the newsletter had taken on a slightly different tone. For the past few months, it had drawn him in, encouraging him in his status as a veteran.

A lot of folks thought he should continually want to talk about his life in the Marines. Kids wanted to know how many bad guys he'd "smoked." A woman at the first responder BBQ last summer had wanted to know who he'd had back home to miss him during his time overseas, and when he said there was no one then or now, she'd started to drape herself over him like she was melted cheese. As if there was anything special about him.

Alena understood what living a military life meant in a way most regular people didn't.

After what'd happened with his ex-wife, and then during those last weeks in the service, he didn't want to talk about it. But people thought that was only bluster and kept asking questions. Pressing, like he needed to "get it out."

The manager hemmed and hawed. "You have to understand…"

Alena didn't let him finish whatever he'd been about to say. Hank didn't tell her he'd gone over all this with the guy and was equally unimpressed. "Multiple crimes have been committed on your property today. What about the safety and security of your guests?"

"We have a team of security guards. I've asked them to increase their rounds, for the safety of our guests." He lifted his chin. "But I'm sure these were only isolated events." He cleared his throat. "After all, they seem to all be in proximity of you."

"I'm not checking out."

Hank felt the pull of a smile on his lips. Alena wasn't the kind of woman who backed down. He'd seen it before, and been swept away by her for a moment. Now it was happening again.

The fire in her warmed him. In a way he hadn't felt for a long time. His wife hadn't been like this, which was probably why it'd fallen apart between them. That, and the fact she'd cheated on him while he was in Afghanistan. Like the reality of him being deployed was a surprise she hadn't been prepared for.

Alena reminded him of the time he'd seen his mom stand up to his father. They'd been arguing about something, and she never backed down. Hank hadn't even known what the fight was over, but he'd walked into the kitchen, sweaty from wrestling, to find them yelling. Seconds later they'd been kissing, which to a thirteen-year-old boy was super gross. He'd hightailed it out of there fast. But that fire in his mom's eyes? She'd been a sight to behold.

Alena had that same spark.

In her own way, with her dark features where his mom had been blonde. There was plenty of mystery about this FBI agent. Strength and vulnerability. A temper. The drive to stick out a case to the end.

He didn't want to be taken with her, but who could control it?

Just because he was attracted didn't mean he would do something about it—other than watch her back while she was here. After she left town and returned to Wyoming and her FBI life, she would be a fond memory. He hoped.

"Fine." The manager practically spat the word out. "I'll get you a room on the fourth floor."

Hank realized he'd tuned them out, deep in his thoughts. The manager whirled around and headed across the parking lot. Alena turned to Hank. "They value their guests' *privacy*?"

Hank shrugged. "A lot of rich folk vacation here. It's a popular spot. They even have a movie festival in the spring." He tended to avoid town that week if he wasn't working.

"Great." She shifted her weight from foot to foot.

With the sarge still in the room not done collecting evidence yet, Hank made an executive decision. "I need to let Dax stretch his legs. Want to walk with us?"

Alena nodded.

He leashed Dax and got him out of the crate. His K-9 partner shook out his body, antsy from being cooped up while Hank worked. His partner knew when something was going on and he wanted to be in the middle of it every time.

"Let's go." Hank started walking.

Dax kept close to his side. They headed for the spot where Brittany had been kidnapped, Alena behind them. He didn't want to go too far away and planned to keep a close eye on her just in case she was targeted again.

It rubbed up against his sensibilities as a cop that he hadn't found the shooter. The guy had to have shot at her and immediately hauled his rifle up and run away. Otherwise, Hank would've seen him. A person determined to kill her would've stuck around to finish the job and make sure she was dead. They'd probably have also killed him, catching him in their crossfire.

Brittany hadn't been killed.

Alena hadn't been shot.

Nothing had been stolen from her room.

Hank glanced over his shoulder. "Seems like there's a lot of threat but not much action."

"What do you mean?"

He explained what he'd just been thinking, then said, "It's like there's no follow-through. Like they're just warnings with no substance."

"But I have to be onto something. Otherwise it wouldn't be worth warning me off," Alena said. "Because they draw attention to themselves by doing that."

"And leave behind evidence."

"Except the hotel has no surveillance. So how do I get a look at whoever broke into my hotel room?" She sighed aloud.

He understood her frustration. It was the same thing he'd felt not finding that shooter and having to turn back to find the victim. Only, she hadn't been in the parking lot. She'd been working the case, talking to Brittany's roommate. Getting information about the fitness tracker so they'd been able to access the GPS location and know where to start looking.

Alena was the kind of woman who might get knocked down, but she came back swinging.

Refusing to let life send her to the ground. That focused determination was admirable.

"We can set up some cameras. In case it happens again." Hank could requisition something from the department that might work.

"Good idea," she said. "I'll have my department run the manager as well. See if anything hinky in his financials might indicate he was being pressured—or paid off—to look the other way while the thefts happen this weekend."

Hank let Dax sniff around the base of a tree. "Anything in the previous cases to suggest staff involvement?"

"No." She sighed again.

"Doesn't mean it didn't happen. Just means the FBI didn't get wind of it." He wanted to poke a little, see some of that fire.

It worked. Alena set her hands on her hips. "Excuse me?"

He chuckled.

"You said that on purpose." She slapped at his shoulder gently, but it had strength to it.

This woman could stand on her own two feet despite the fear.

"Let's get you settled in another room and you can get some rest. We can—"

Dax went on alert.

What is it, buddy? Hank didn't speak aloud or he'd risk distracting his dog asking for attention that would take him away from whatever he'd spotted.

Alena shifted closer to stand by him. "Someone is watching us."

Hank moved both himself and Dax into a protective stance. "Let's get back to the room."

Then he would find whoever it was.

FIVE

The emergency room doors slid open. Alena strode up to the desk attendant, pocketing her rental car keys and pulling out her badge. Her arm felt weightier than it should, but she was exhausted. She'd slept barely two hours after half the Sundown Valley Police Department had come by the hotel to see the damage and meet the FBI agent working in their town.

Thankfully, Hank's boss, the chief of police, hadn't showed up before they were done processing the scene, collecting evidence, and Alena could finally pack a bag and move to a new room. She'd had to answer enough questions as it was.

Out in the woods, she'd only *felt* someone watching, but Hank had walked her to gather her things and she'd opted for rest, like he'd suggested. So tired, she'd been seeing double. Not the time to go looking for shadows.

Trying to sleep while her mind wrestled with the strands of what was going on, trying to tie them together in a way that made sense. She should call her dad and check on him but wanted to wait until he'd be awake.

"Can I help you?"

Alena blinked. "I'm Special Agent Sanchez. I'd like to speak with Brittany Hattenden, if she's available for a visit."

The attendant's eyes widened at Alena's badge. Not the first time she'd had that reaction from a civilian, but this was a small town. She had no intention of throwing federal weight around. Most of what had happened since she'd arrived here was the jurisdiction of local police—and that was how Alena wanted it to stay. Brittany would figure out soon enough who she was, and if she was a suspect, the group would know the FBI was onto them.

For the sake of expediency, she used her badge to get through the door. Later she would use it to take down the whole group.

"Thanks." The desk attendant lowered the phone. "She 'checked out.' Like this is a hotel." She shook her head. "Anyway, she left an hour ago. She's not here."

Alena slid her badge into her jacket pocket. "Thanks."

She headed back to the car, taking her keys out as she walked. Alena had even dressed the part of an FBI agent today, complete with a vest under her jacket. Black khakis and a white shirt. There was no point in taking chances if whoever had shot at her the day before was still out there. It had to be one of the group that was stealing jewelry. Nothing else made sense—and her ASAC would agree with her. When she got around to telling him.

The risk they'd pull her from the assignment wasn't worth taking.

For her own sake, she needed to do this.

Her phone started to ring. She fought back the reaction, not needing anyone to see her jump out of her skin in a public place.

Alena kept going to the car, refusing to cower to fear or outlandish ideas like car bombs and more snipers. She turned the engine on and let the call connect to the speakers through Bluetooth. The number was local. "Special Agent Sanchez."

"This is the Sundown Valley Police Department." The voice was female, but of course her mind went to Officer Miller. "The chief has requested you come in for a meeting."

Alena waited for the *if you're available*, which apparently wasn't coming as the caller didn't add that part. She figured she might as well get it over with—and as far as safe places, that was pretty high up on the list. "Of course. I'll be right there."

"Thank you." The lady hung up.

Sundown Valley PD wasn't far. Alena spotted Hank's K-9 vehicle parked outside, but that didn't mean he was there. It was his day off, after all. His idea to meet up hadn't come to anything. After she'd pretty much kicked out the police department, and the resort manager gave her a key for another room, she'd headed for bed rather than snap at anyone else just because she was tired. They hadn't confirmed those plans for breakfast, which was fine by her because she'd have been miserable due to the exhaustion anyway.

Alena headed in and found the desk sergeant. She flashed her badge. "Alena Sanchez."

"Come with me." He hopped off his stool, walked her around the corner to the end of the hall and knocked on a glass door. "Chief?"

"Send her in, Sarge."

The man behind the desk wore a uniform with a white shirt and chief pins on his collar. Wire-rimmed glasses. A mustache and dark gray hair, thick and styled on his head. He stood as she entered, and Alena held out her hand. "Sanchez."

"Good to meet you." He shook and sat. "Chief Willa." He waved her to a chair.

"Anything come of evidence collection?" She sat.

"The shooting, the kidnapper's van, or your hotel room?"

Alena hesitated. "Yes."

He grinned. "Sure, if you wait two to three weeks for fingerprint analysis to come back." He leaned back in his chair. "Just another day at the office for you? Getting shot at. Having your room ransacked?"

"Not exactly. Why do you say that?"

He studied her. "You seem pretty unflustered."

Alena shrugged. "I've had a few hours to think on it." And the only thing she could control right now was her own reaction to what was going on.

"Conclusion?"

"I need a way to find out if the kidnapping, the shooting and the break-in are connected to the case I've been working." Alena tapped her fingers on the arm of the chair.

"So what's your plan?" Chief Willa seemed like a capable leader. She liked the guy—and the insignia patch on the sleeve of his dark jacket hung up to her right. Maybe one day she wouldn't find herself surrounded by military guys, but was that even what she wanted?

For good or ill, that was how her life had worked out.

Alena said, "I'd like to talk to Brittany Hattenden, find out if the kidnapper said or did anything." Given his impression on the time it would take to get back fingerprint analysis on her hotel room, she wasn't going to bother asking about the van. "Any evidence your people have found that might point to who the kidnapper was?"

He shook his head. "Stolen van. Belonged to a construction business, anyone employed there used it. We're checking alibis of all their staff members, but a lot of their employees are paid with cash, so they may not even be listed on the payroll. It could be unlikely we'll find everyone who could've used it—and nearly anyone in town could've had access to it."

"He might have taken off his mask at some point. Or said something to Brittany that can get us closer to an ID on who he is," Alena said. "If one of the crew double-crossed her, she might be angry enough to implicate them."

Chief Willa nodded. "Do you think maybe it's possible Brittany set the whole thing up as a ruse to throw you off? Make it look like the hit on you was related to the kidnapping and not getting rid of the fed on their tail."

"It's possible. She wasn't badly hurt, and she seemed more mad about it than anything else when we saw her yesterday at the hospital." Alena frowned. Apparently, Hank hadn't spared any detail in his report to the chief. She didn't know if that said more about the kind of boss this man was, or about Hank himself. "All I have right now are theories."

He started to speak. A dog barked in the hall. She turned to see Dax trot in and come right up to her. Alena held her hands out. The K-9 put his chin on her palms, so she scratched his fur. "Good morning to you."

Chief Willa chuckled.

Hank stood at the door, frowning. "Don't turn my police dog into a pet."

She resisted the urge to lean down, get nose to nose with the dog and say, *But he's so cute, yes he is.* Probably that wouldn't go down well. She patted the side of Dax's neck and dropped her hands back to her lap.

Hank said, "Dax, heel."

Dax spun around and went to sit beside Hank's leg.

Alena glanced at Hank. "Brittany checked out of the hospital this morning. We need to track her down."

He nodded. "Let's talk to the roommate while we're at the resort. We need more information from both of them."

"Good idea," Chief Willa said. "Miller, you keep an eye on our FBI friend. Make sure nothing happens that would be bad for the department, yeah?"

Alena smiled. A leader who could also function as a solid politician? Her dad was too much of a marine to swing both ways on that pendulum. This guy was more like her ASAC. Speaking of which... "I should call my boss. Update him on everything that's happened."

Chief Willa picked up his pen. "You do that. Have them call me, too. Got it?" When she nodded, he said, "Top priorities are finding the guy who kidnapped Brittany and then left her on the side of the mountain. And keeping you safe until we figure out who is targeting *you*."

Alena might appreciate the sentiment, but she also didn't much like the sound of that. She was a cop, not the victim or a witness—except that wasn't true, was it?

The shooting could just be an elaborate way of getting her attention. Making her duck, scared enough she ran away from this case. Trashing her room. All of it said she was close to something. Not that she was in danger, necessarily.

If she cut and run at the first sign of trouble every time, what kind of agent would she be?

Not the kind her dad would be proud of.

Hank was all in to figure out if Alena was in danger and what was going on at the resort. "Copy that, Chief."

Alena shot him some kind of look he couldn't decipher. Surprised he wanted to wade in? After he'd made sure she was settled last night, he'd searched the woods around the resort with Dax, but they hadn't found anything.

Surely, she didn't think he would allow the daughter of the marine corps leader he respected most to be hurt when he could do something to protect her? No way.

Even if she'd been closed off since her hotel room had been broken into didn't mean he'd leave her exposed to danger. He intended to find out what was going on here.

Chief Willa picked up his pen. "Officer Miller, accompany Special Agent Sanchez for the foreseeable future and we'll see what the two of you come up with." Willa glanced at Alena. "And come Monday morning…"

"I'll either be out of your hair—" she lifted her hands "—or we'll know for sure everything is part of my FBI investigation, not a local case."

"I'd rather my town wasn't overrun with feds." Willa winked. "So let's see what you two can do over the next couple of days, okay?"

Hank nodded. "Yes, sir."

Dax barked.

Alena stood. "Thank you, Chief."

They walked side by side to the alcove where his desk was tucked away out of the busy hall, along with a crate for Dax.

Hank grabbed his jacket. "Let's head to the resort and talk to Brittany—if she's there—

and her roommate. I'll drive." He used his desk phone to call the manager and make sure neither of them had checked out. Who knew where Brittany had gone after she'd left the hospital? She could be anywhere.

Once in the vehicle, Alena scrolled her phone on the drive, giving him the idea she wasn't interested in small talk. Maybe she was even more exhausted than he was, considering how easily she'd agreed to leave her rental car. Meanwhile, Dax stood at the side of his crate where he could sniff the wind coming through the open back window.

Eventually, Alena dropped her phone on her lap. "You know what I don't get?"

"What's that?" He gripped the wheel and turned a corner, wanting, more than he probably should, for her to tell him *anything*. He was drawn to this woman, and not just because he wanted to protect her.

She, on the other hand, seemed determined to solve the case and that was it.

He should follow her lead and keep this professional.

"Why kidnap her if she's part of their crew?"

Hank said, "And I can't help but wonder if the roommate is in on it."

"Agreed," Alena said. "I've got my office checking her ID so we'll know if it's really

Carol or if the woman we met is an imposter. Maybe they're both pretending to be someone they're not."

"Or she's innocent and has nothing to do with the Brittany imposter and the scheme for this weekend."

She nodded slowly. "If they're both involved, there's no way they'll just admit it in a statement. Which is probably why Brittany was cagey yesterday and then split from the hospital today."

"Maybe the plan is to stay in denial." Hank frowned. "Forget the whole thing happened and avoid making a statement to the police."

"Why stick around?"

"Desperation or something else." Hank thought for a second. "We need a way to surveil them. If they're still here, planning on sticking out the conference."

Maybe she was out of sorts because her cover had been blown. Alena might have preferred keeping her anonymity and working undercover, but that wasn't how things had shaken out. She was in danger now—whether she was prepared to admit it or not.

But why had Brittany been taken from here, just to shove her off a cliff and have her survive?

Maybe some kind of threat...

He spotted Carol in the forecourt when they

pulled up, walking Brittany's dog. "Check it out." He pointed at the woman and the pet.

Alena shoved her door open. "That means Brittany didn't check out—or she'd have taken her dog with her."

In the hospital, Hank had heard Brittany call the animal "Kitty," but wasn't sure that was the Chihuahua's actual name. It seemed more than a little odd. He leashed Dax and let him out of the crate, following over to where Alena made a beeline for Carol. "Hey, how's Brittany doing this morning?"

Carol lifted her chin, the dog pulling on the leash in her hand to get to a bench so she could sniff around.

"How are you doing, watching her dog? It's nice of you to do that."

"You're a fed. I heard you got shot at." Carol eyed her. "And everyone at breakfast was talking about cops in the parking lot last night."

Hank kept Dax on the opposite side of Alena, away from the little dog.

"Yeah, that was about me." Alena lifted her hands, a sheepish look on her face. "Guess I picked the wrong place to spend the weekend, huh?"

Carol didn't seem convinced. And she hadn't answered Alena's question about Brittany.

Hank said, "Is Ms. Hattenden in your room?"

Carol nodded. "She's taking a nap."

"I'm interested to know what people think about everything that happened." The rumor mill could be a powerful way to collect information. It wasn't admissible in court, but in this town it could lead to a person of interest.

Carol shrugged. "How should I know? I've been with Brittany since early this morning, taking care of her."

"Is she doing okay?" Alena pretty much repeated her opening question. "What did the doctor say about her injuries?"

"She's fine, thanks to you guys, I guess."

"That's good." Alena gave her a polite smile Hank didn't believe one bit. "I was worried after Dax found her on the side of that hill."

"Is it possible to get a statement from Brittany?" Hank asked. "The department requires one after a crime has been committed. After all, we don't want this guy to get away with what he did. Or do the same to someone else. The outcome might be a lot worse next time."

Carol slid out her phone and glanced at the screen. "I can see if she's awake, but she was sleeping pretty heavily when I stepped out to walk her dog. She'll be groggy when she wakes. Then getting ready for the fundraising event tonight. She insisted on going. Otherwise, whoever kidnapped her might think they won."

Hank had no idea if that was something Brittany had said to Carol, or if there was no truth in this entire conversation.

"I saw posters for the event," Alena said. "Isn't it a mixer? And they're raising money for a national shelter foundation."

"They remove dogs from those shelters with high kill rates and house them until they can be adopted." Carol shrugged one shoulder. "It's the charity the host company chose."

A plan began to form in Hank's mind. Still, he said, "Ms. Hattenden really needs to make a statement to the police. After all, a kidnapper took her. He could have killed her."

They needed to speak to Brittany—Elizabeth—if she hadn't left, but just observing her mingling could also provide valuable information—if she'd stuck around to follow through with the job. Even the police hadn't been able to get a statement from her at the hospital.

If they could observe both of these women, they might be able to draw out the kidnapper—and Brittany/Elizabeth's partners.

Alena's cover might've been blown, but Hank could use that as a distraction. They'd be looking for her, not him and Dax.

Carol said, "I should go back inside. You can check back later and see if Brittany has time."

She scooped the dog from the planter where he'd been digging and strode to the lobby doors.

Hank watched her walk away. Dax sat and leaned against his leg. "That dog is definitely comfortable with her."

"Like they know each other?"

He shrugged. "You think Brittany will even be here later, like, at that event?" Hank glanced at Alena. "If I was her, pretty sure I'd suddenly realize I needed to leave town."

Alena sighed. "If she does that, it doesn't help me figure out if she's really a suspect in my case. She might be connected to the murder of the real Brittany Hattenden, but until my team confirms that I can't bring her in."

"We need to get eyes on her."

"Great. Except my cover is blown and the manager doesn't want any more FBI operations on his property." Alena folded her arms. "Unless I can somehow get an invite to that fundraiser as a civilian, in which case I'd be back undercover." She winced. "It's a risk, but not everyone here has seen my face."

Hank felt his mouth stretch into a smile.

"You can get me in?" Her brows rose and mischief lit her eyes.

"I'm the local K-9 officer. I got an invite in the mail months ago, but I stuffed it in the drawer." Hank figured that would dispel anyone's belief she wasn't connected to law enforcement. He hoped that would offer her some protection. "I think we should take them up on their kind offer and represent the police department. You can be my plus-one."

"Sounds like we're tracking down Brittany tonight so we can see what she's up to."

Hank nodded. "If she's going to talk to us, it might be when she's relaxed and having a good time."

"Or we might catch a thief in the act."

If he could spend more time with Alena, not only would he do the job the chief had assigned him and be able to keep her safe, but he'd also glean more about this case. Two ways to deal with the same problem, as far as he could see. With the added bonus that he'd be doing what he felt like he should be—the thing missing from his relationship with Evan. Looking out for someone who meant something to him.

Alena had come here alone to prove to her bosses that Brittany was involved. Hank didn't know if she was a victim, or the perpetrator, or both, but he wasn't going to find out any other way than by sticking with Alena.

For as long as she let him.

SIX

Alena walked into the fundraising gala and over to Hank, who held on to Dax's leash. While she'd hit a tiny local boutique and found a dress to wear, he had taken the K-9 to a dog wash place in town so he didn't smell like dirt. The whole time she'd been looking over her shoulder. Like a gunman would start shooting, or someone would throw her in a van.

She needed to work this case. Be proactive rather than reacting because things kept happening with no letup. Realizing how key tonight might be made her want to pray they were successful. However, she couldn't trust it would do any good when she couldn't see evidence God had even been listening lately.

Hank lifted a hand to tug at the collar of his shirt, secured by a tie. "Wow. Nice dress."

"Thank you." No one had complimented her about her appearance in a long time. Hank Miller wasn't like the guys she worked with. He seemed more down-to-earth. There was a quiet strength about him that she appreciated.

He turned to step into the main ballroom of the resort event center, and she got a look at the fit of his suit. "That's not rented, is it?"

"It was in my closet." He stopped just inside the ballroom.

Alena went to the side opposite Dax. "Your closet?"

He shrugged one shoulder. "My parents— before they died—were on the board of several charities. As part of the trust they handed down to Evan and me, we have to show our faces at some events every year. Although, usually I just write a check and stay home."

"But the invite you had for this one was about Dax, right?" He'd left her name at the entry table as his plus-one.

"Right. So I need to do a lap of the room with the four-legged hero and let people see him, talk about why donating to shelters is so important, and generally do what I said I would."

"A man who keeps his word?" Alena grinned. "Be still my heart."

Hank chuckled. "If I see Brittany, I'll text you."

"Copy that." She responded that way because Alena had no intention of slipping into anything personal. Even though she was the one who'd made that quip, and so far Hank had done nothing but keep things professional between them, she couldn't help being attracted to him.

Her last relationship had ended with her boyfriend in handcuffs—hers. Dragging him to the FBI so the US attorney could bring federal charges might have helped close the case she'd been working. But it hadn't done any favors for her personally, or professionally. Especially not when the charges had eventually been dropped. The smirk on his lawyer's face when the case had been dismissed was something Alena would never forget.

She'd had to claw her way back to professional respect, and that had been a long road.

Alena circled the room far enough to get herself a glass of water, which she sipped at while she tried not to make it obvious that she was searching for Brittany in the crowd. She'd talked to her ASAC while she'd tried on dresses, updating him on everything that had happened so far. There had been a development in another case, and Alena had local police protection, so he'd trusted her to handle what she could and let him know if that changed.

She sipped from the glass and scanned the room. Doctors and hospital administrators rubbed elbows with pharmaceutical executives. Brittany wasn't there, and neither was Carol. Yet.

Since she and her ASAC had agreed that her chief suspects now knew Alena was an FBI agent, they figured that would put Brittany on her best behavior. Unfortunately, that meant anything she had come here to do might be on hold. So, if Alena watched her, waiting for her to do something that would incriminate her, it was likely to never happen.

Unless the crew *had* to steal jewels this weekend.

Brittany had been kidnapped. Whether the woman wanted to admit that to the police or not. The cops here had been trying to get her to give them a statement after she'd blown off Hank and Alena at the hospital.

A suited man in his late thirties with dark hair he'd shaved close to his head and a red silk tie nodded as he passed her. "Good evening."

Alena lifted her glass in a salute. "Yes, it is."

He glanced at her for a second longer but kept going.

She wasn't sure what his attention meant but filed away in her mind a few key details about him that she might need to remember later. The scar on the side of his neck just above his collar. The way he'd moved as he'd walked away, and that gold watch on his wrist.

Alena didn't like treating everyone in the world with suspicion, but she was working right now. It might be harmless interest, or merely politeness, but she had learned the hard way not to take the risk.

Across the room, Hank had stopped to speak with three men whose attire indicated they had deep pockets. The charity was likely relying on these men to fund their activities for the year. Looking around, she could spot those who were local, like the mayor. The conference attendees seemed to be here more for the schmoozing than workshops or academics. They'd turned out tonight in all their flash.

Dax sat obediently beside Hank. Even though she figured he would probably much prefer being outside running around playing right now, the dog's professionalism shone through in his demeanor. Hank handled himself like a professional, too, and despite what he'd said about events like this, he seemed to be a natural with the people here as much as he was with Dax. The kind of guy she had given up on finding.

It was too bad that Chadwell had taught her the pain of betrayal. These days she was just focusing on her career and not trying to add someone to her life.

Otherwise, she would be very interested in a man like Hank. Except for the fact their lives had them hundreds of miles from each other, he seemed like an amazing guy. Given the distance, it wasn't like it would work anyway, even if she was willing to give up all the lessons she had learned.

Alena even held her father at arm's length since Chadwell. She couldn't help being ashamed of the mistake and feared her father's reaction.

All that did was spark in her a note of grief, but she didn't want to fall into that when she was supposed to be working. It wasn't her father's fault how she felt. Not after everything that'd happened in the past few months. It was just that the way he had raised her meant not a whole lot of affection had built between them. He'd treated her like one of his soldiers, which was exactly who Hank was.

Now?

Alena couldn't think about that.

She spotted Brittany across the room, engaged in conversation with a man in his seventies with a much younger wife on his arm.

As soon as Brittany broke off from them, Alena planned to intercept her. She needed the woman to tell her as much as she could remember about the man who'd kidnapped her. It was possible Brittany was acting under duress, then and since, and the kidnapping had been some kind of threat. A harsh reminder of who was in charge—a thought that caused her to shiver. Alena knew well what that felt like.

If she was going to figure this out, she needed all the information she could get about these people and what was going on.

Brittany's gaze drifted. Alena looked over to where the young woman had focused her attention for a second. The man who had said good evening to her was now facing off with Brittany's roommate, Carol.

As Alena watched, he grabbed her by the arm and forced her to walk with him out of the room. Alena was going to have to forget Brittany for a moment and help Carol.

Alena sent a quick text to Hank and then followed the two of them. Carol had looked scared. Brittany had glanced at the man. Were they working together? Was this the kidnapper? If need be, she could draw the weapon in the ankle holster under the skirt of her dress. But if she could help it, she would do as much of this as possible without her gun.

She peered around the open doorway first. Carol and the man were halfway down the hall, in a heated conversation. The man shoved Carol up against the wall, his forearm across the front of her throat.

Alena called out, "Let her go!" and started running toward them.

The man pushed off Carol, glanced at Alena and raced away down the hall.

Hank brushed past her, Dax right next to him. "We've got this. Stay with her."

The man turned the corner at the end of the hallway. Hank raced after him, giving Dax a little slack in the leash so if his dog put on a sudden burst of speed, he wouldn't be in danger of feeling resistance from Hank's hold on him.

"Look." Dax knew what that command meant and pulled back on his speed.

They slowed for the corner, Hank looked first and then they resumed their chase after the man. He drew his weapon as he ran. Just in case.

This was a far better use of their skills than working a room of people with money, representing the department and drumming up support for a charity. That was valuable work, but Hank and Dax were the kinds of males who craved action.

Up ahead, the man punched his way through a pair of exit doors on the quiet side of the event center. Hank didn't slow down as he did the same, catching the door before it closed. A few people milled around outside on a heated patio with their drinks. Making connections with their peers—business and personal.

He'd seen what that man had been doing to Brittany's roommate. Alena's text had come through a second after he'd seen her move toward the hallway. He'd been explaining to the people he was talking to why he needed to withdraw from the conversation before she'd even texted him.

Maybe he was just entirely too focused on her. Even at the periphery of his awareness, he'd seen that guy walk past her. Say something briefly. The same man who had then dragged out Carol. The fact this might be a distraction so Brittany could get up to something while their backs were turned occurred to him. But there was nothing he could do about that right now.

Not with a suspect in his sights.

The man raced away, running fast around the side of the building along a wide cobblestone pathway. To the left, siding stretched up to the roof of the building. On the right an expanse of landscaped grass was sprinkled with patches of snow. Trees, benches and other pathways intersected the resort grounds.

Dax put on a burst of speed.

Hank rewarded the energy by saying, "Go get him, Dax. Get him."

His dog didn't have the temperament to work

exclusively in takedowns or protection. Dax did not want to spend his days tackling suspects or dragging them out of hiding places. But finding a child in the woods? It was one of Dax's favorite things. When they went a long stretch between Search and Rescue calls, Hank would work with the local church youth group and do some training so that Dax could keep his skills sharp by finding the teens who had been "lost" and alerting Hank of their location.

Hank shifted to run on the grass, since dress shoes and cobblestone didn't mix. Dax didn't feel the effects. The guy running up ahead apparently had treads on the soles of his shoes, because he was *fast*. Hank might not catch him.

The guy reached the parking lot, and Hank sped up as much as he could. But it wasn't fast enough. The man jumped into a car and drove away before Hank stepped onto the asphalt.

He took in as much detail as he could about the vehicle and the license plate, getting a partial in the dim light. A local tag.

Dax barked.

He knew his quarry was gone. "We'll find him."

Hank patted his dog's head and then led him around to the front door, where he found the manager and asked for water for Dax. While he was waiting, Hank pulled out his phone and called the officer on duty at the police department. He explained what had happened and gave all the information he could think of.

"You need a uniformed officer?"

"Not right now," Hank said. "I'll find out if the victim needs medical assistance."

Then they would locate Brittany.

The manager came over with a bowl and bottled water. Hank hung up with the duty officer and thanked him. As soon as Dax was done drinking, he walked his K-9 to the hallway where he'd left Alena and Carol. He found them on a couch, talking quietly. Brittany's roommate had a drink of her own, which she held in both hands.

Alena glanced up as he approached. He shook his head and she mouthed the word *same*. Apparently the roommate wasn't being too forthcoming.

Since Alena had seen the man's face, she could at least look at mug shots of the local suspects and try to identify him. Added to the information he'd gotten from the car, they could potentially locate the guy. They didn't necessarily need Carol's help. But the fact two women had been victims in the span of two days presented a pattern that said they were connected more than just by happening to be roommates for the weekend.

He pulled back and didn't get any closer to Carol, not wanting to come across the same as the man who had accosted her. "How are you feeling? We can have an EMT check you out, if you'd like."

Carol shook her head. "I don't need help."

Alena shifted on the seat beside her. "See, that's the problem. Because, on the other hand, *I* do need help. A crime was committed, and if that man isn't found then he will only continue hurting people. So I need you to help me, Carol. Tell me what's going on."

Hank figured if that didn't work, he could ask her if she minded that the next person could even be killed. Did she want that on her conscience? It was always a mystery precisely how much pressure caused a person to finally open up when they were not inclined to do it. But there was also not any point in becoming belligerent with a witness who was also a victim. That type of police officer wasn't an asset to any department—local or federal.

Carol said, "I don't know who he was."

"That doesn't matter." Hank shifted his stance and Dax lay down next to him. "We have enough information to find him on our own. And when he tells us what you've done in order to make a deal and save himself jail time, we'll know for sure that you're lying."

"Okay. I know who he is." Carol squared her shoulders. Not a bad thing that she was feeling defensive, because proving they were wrong meant she was talking. "But you can't tell Brittany anything. I don't want her to know about this."

Hank didn't know what to make of that. Could be she didn't want her roommate distracted—but from what? "Who is he?"

Carol blanched. "I can't tell you!"

Frustrated, Hank said, "You just said you know him. You have to tell us."

Carol whimpered.

"We know she's not really Brittany Hattenden," Alena said. "Her name is Elizabeth, and you knew each other before you came here. Didn't you?"

"I…" Carol swallowed. "Do I need a lawyer?"

Hank suspected Carol was trying to save herself. "You're not under arrest. Yet." He sighed. "Let me guess, you don't want the hassle of this getting complicated? You just want everything to go away. Like it never happened." Too bad they didn't know what. They needed Carol to say more than she intended—or enough they could catch her in a lie. "Or you need things to continue without us messing it up?"

Carol said nothing.

"You need to start talking, Carol." Hank widened his stance, wanting to be in his work uniform rather than this suit. "Tell us everything."

She glanced between them.

"News flash." Alena brushed back hair from her forehead. "Things you've done have a nasty habit of coming back to bite you, and the past will never quite let you go."

Carol's eyes filled with tears.

"What are you and Brittany involved in?" Alena softened her tone. "If you're in trouble, we can help you."

Carol shook her head. "It's too late."

"I know what it's like to realize that you've made a terrible mistake." Alena cleared her throat. "It's never too late to do the right thing."

Hank studied Alena for a second. He made a note to ask her about what she'd said, if she might trust him enough to share something so clearly painful. And that didn't take away from the respect he had for her. It actually strengthened it, knowing she'd been through something.

Alena might know what it was like to make a mistake that had real consequences and have to scrape together a life afterward.

He said, "Brittany was kidnapped over this. Your life could be in danger, Carol." Just like Alena's seemed to be.

"She's back now." Carol brushed her hands

over the skirt on her knees. "She wasn't hurt that badly."

"Why did that man shove you against the wall?" Alena leaned forward slightly. "Why was he trying to hurt you?"

Carol swallowed. More tears gathered in her eyes. "He said if I told anyone, he would kill me."

"Told what? What does he want from you?" Alena shook her head. "What's going on?"

Carol sniffed. "He's been blackmailing me."

SEVEN

"You can have a seat over there." Alena pointed to the desk and chair in her room. She'd ended up two floors below Carol and Brittany's suite because that was all the manager, Nathanial Bremerton, had—or so he'd said. They'd searched for Brittany but found her still with the crowd in the gala event. Hank had his chief send over an officer in plain clothes to watch her and report to them if she left the busy room.

Hank pulled the chair back from the desk and Carol sat. Alena got her a bottled water from the fridge. "Here you go."

Hank let Dax off his leash with a command to lie down. The dog wandered over to the wall and slumped onto his side, his back to it. Alena wanted to be distracted by them but now wasn't the time.

"Thanks." Carol's hand shook but she got the bottle open.

Alena sat on the end of the bed so she could

be eye level with Carol and not come across as intimidating by standing over her the way she might during an interrogation. The adrenaline seeing that man shove Carol lingered, along with the memories it had triggered.

Hank leaned against the wall with his arms folded across his chest. Alena wanted to change out of the gown she was wearing, probably as much as he wanted to lose the suit in favor of jeans and a T-shirt. All she'd seen him wear so far were his work uniform and this suit.

It made her wonder what he looked like when he wasn't on duty.

Alena refocused her thoughts on Carol now that the woman had taken a moment to compose herself. She leaned forward, forearms on her knees. "I can understand how you might be reluctant to speak with me, knowing I'm an FBI agent. But in order to figure out what's happening here, I need to know everything you know about that man who attacked you and what Brittany is involved with that might have gotten her kidnapped yesterday."

Carol lowered the water from her lips. "I don't know what kind of scam they're into. I'm just Brittany's roommate. I'm supposed to watch and keep my mouth shut."

"Like a gag order?" Hank asked.

She'd mentioned blackmail, but immediately

clammed up when they'd asked about it. Now Carol said, "They took my phone and gave me a flip phone."

"Who are they? Are they watching you and Brittany?"

"They're watching us. But I'm supposed to keep tabs on her and report in."

And yet Brittany had been kidnapped. Alena said, "You mentioned you were being black-mailed, Carol. I need you to tell us about that."

"The man in the hallway, the one you chased…?"

"Yes?" Hank said. "He jumped into a car and got away, but I noted a partial license plate and Alena saw his face. So it's only a matter of time before we ID him, and then find him. If he threatened you, then you won't have to worry about him much longer, but we would find him a lot faster and use less resources if you just tell us who he is."

Alena shifted in her seat. Yes, she'd seen the man's face. But in that moment, she also felt everything Carol had been going through. Because Alena had been through the same thing with her ex.

Could she ID the man?

Alena hoped so. But her mind was full of memories right now. The night Chadwell had found out she'd realized who he really was and was about to arrest him, he'd lost it and nearly killed her.

Thankfully, he'd left her for dead. Alena hadn't told anyone at work what she'd suspected about Chadwell. She had planned to bring him in quietly, but not calling for backup before she confronted him had been a big mistake. Part of what had put her on probation in the first place. In the end, it was a couple of her colleagues who'd tracked him down and graciously allowed Alena to arrest him.

"His name is Matthew, but I don't know his last name or anything about him." Carol swallowed. "We met a month ago. I thought he loved me."

"You need to give us more than that, Carol." Alena tried to bite back the frustration, even though she knew well enough how abusive relationships worked, and how it'd messed with her head. None of this made sense. "You're tied up in whatever they're up to. Which makes you an accomplice to any crime they commit."

Carol sniffed. "I was supposed to text him every time Brittany left, and when she came back. I had to tell him anytime she contacted their partner. I was supposed to take photos of her messages and send them to him."

Hank frowned. "But you only met Brittany yesterday?"

Alena wanted to know more about the partner, and Matthew.

Carol blanched. "Okay. I've known her for a while. We met a couple of weeks ago, after I met Matthew at a bar." Embarrassment pinked her cheeks. "I think they used to be a thing—Matthew and Elizabeth. I don't know about the other guy. I just want out of this."

As far as Alena could tell, she was neck-deep in it.

"You were keeping tabs on her for him?" She figured that could mean a number of things. Matthew making sure she was out of the way at the appropriate moment. Or making sure she wasn't betraying them.

Carol nodded.

Alena said, "Is Matthew the same person who kidnapped her?"

"I don't know." Carol raised one hand then dropped it back to her lap. "She won't even talk to me about what happened. She won't speak to me at all. Like I betrayed *her* or something." Tears fell down Carol's cheeks. "I thought he loved me."

Alena had said those same words. Only to herself though. Never to anyone else. "Carol, we need your help. We need Elizabeth to talk about what she's involved in, who kidnapped her and why they did it. And we need to know what they're doing here—why she's pretending to be this 'Brittany' woman."

Carol said, "Then arrest her. Isn't that what you're going to do with me?"

"Unfortunately, we don't have enough evidence to do that." Alena had a way that they could get it. Then her team at the FBI would have everything they needed to bring down this ring of thieves and forgers—assuming Alena was still right about Brittany's involvement.

"It isn't like I can help you," Carol said. "Whatever Elizabeth is doing, I don't know how to stop them. I don't even know what it is. Matthew wouldn't tell me. He just said we were going to be rich after this weekend."

Alena steadied her gaze. "I don't need you to stop them, Carol. That's my job."

This woman might be an innocent dragged into this, but it could also be an act.

Hank spoke up from the other side of the room. "Does Elizabeth know that Alena is after her and this crew? Has she said anything to you, Carol?"

"She was ranting about the police being up in her business earlier. But she didn't mention your name, or anything. Just that this was all going to fall apart probably." Carol sniffed. "I told Matthew, but I don't think he cares."

Alena wondered if both women weren't under

duress, perhaps by the men who were part of their group. But was it just the four of them, or more? She was about to ask where they could find Matthew when Hank said, "Carol, do you know who might have broken into Alena's hotel room?"

The other woman frowned.

He said, "Who shot at Alena on the street, right after Elizabeth was kidnapped?"

"How should I know?" Carol gaped. "It was probably Matthew's partner."

"So Matthew was the one who took Elizabeth," Alena said. "Was it to scare her?"

"How do I know? You have to believe me, I don't know anything."

"Our conclusions will be based on the evidence. Not what you want us to believe." Hank lowered his hands and tucked them in his front pockets. In the suit, he almost looked like an FBI agent. Alena could believe they might be partners in this. But why would a partner of hers bring up the threat against her when they needed to focus on taking down Elizabeth and her friends?

Alena needed to get this conversation back on track. "Carol, you need to be truthful with us."

Carol said, "I have no idea why they did any of this."

"And yet you're here, in the middle of it all,

being blackmailed." Hank shrugged. "People aren't blackmailed because they don't know anything."

Unless she was simply a woman being used. Like Alena had been.

"Why can't you guys just leave me out of this?" Carol glanced between them. Looking for an ally—or whoever she thought she could manipulate. "I'm the innocent victim here."

Alena glanced over at Hank. He shot her a look that clearly said he didn't believe Carol was quite so innocent as she claimed.

Alena figured she would take a more middle-ground approach and see how that went. "If you are innocent, then I'd like to give you a chance to prove that to us."

Carol bristled. "How?"

"We need you to get Elizabeth talking." Alena usually got one reaction to this request before she managed to convince a person that it was their only chance to prove their innocence. "When you do, we're going to listen in and record everything."

"You want me to wear a wire?"

Hank rarely used confidential informants or persons of interest to get the suspect talking. However, even he knew that they no longer used an actual wire. "I think it's Bluetooth now."

Alena nodded. "That's right. We connect to your phone and Elizabeth will never know there's a line open, or that we are recording what she's saying."

"However, if you are not up to doing this, we understand." Hank needed to offer her an out because she had to understand she wasn't being forced to cooperate. Carol had to choose because it was in her best interest. She needed to prove she wasn't one of their suspects—just a woman who'd been duped.

He ignored the look Alena shot him. Clearly, she wanted the witness to get her Elizabeth and Elizabeth's other associates. There were certain things that he and Alena were never going to agree on. That was good to know, considering how attracted he was to her. Hank needed to focus on the fact that it wouldn't work between them anyway, even if it was an option.

He'd rather keep questioning Carol and then bring in both her and Elizabeth. After that, he'd get a warrant for Matthew's address. But Alena wanted fake Brittany to incriminate herself first.

It would be unfair to paint everyone in the world with the same brush he used to color his opinion of his ex-wife. She'd cheated on him. Alena might not be that kind of woman. He'd never have the chance to know anyway, considering this was over after the weekend ended, and the case was done, so what did it matter? His heart had already decided that now wasn't the right time to fall for someone else and risk the same thing happening. Maybe it never would be.

Since Alena only had the weekend to do her job, it was better to focus on that. Forget about the rest of it, and his attraction to her. She would be gone in a couple of days and then he wouldn't need to worry about how drawn he was to her.

"We know he hurt you," Alena said. "We also know that you have an opportunity here to do something to help yourself. To get you out of this situation where you're backed up to a wall with an arm against your throat." Her voice thickened.

Hank studied her without making it obvious he was watching. Again, he caught a tone in her voice. Something she didn't want anyone to know. There was more to this than Alena had either told him or admitted to Carol.

He didn't think she knew more than she was saying, he just had the impression this was more about something Alena had been through in the past.

Alena continued. "Because, Carol, the alternative is that you find yourself swept up in an FBI raid. Arrested as an accomplice and facing charges you wouldn't have had to face otherwise. Those are your two options, and it's your choice."

Hank knew she was right. And when they had Elizabeth in cuffs, they'd give her the same choice. Back in the hospital, Alena had been trying to maintain her cover—not pushing too hard—trying to see what a soft approach would get them.

Apparently, she was done with that.

"I have nothing to do with this." The reddening bruises across Carol's throat might need medical attention, but she'd refused when they'd asked her if she'd wanted to have it looked at. In a way, she'd reacted similarly to the way Elizabeth did after the kidnapping. Carol wanted to do anything and everything she could to get over it as fast as possible. Almost in denial about how bad the situation was.

It seemed like two men had two women under pressure.

Hank wanted to know what the truth was.

"And yet, you're right in the middle of it." Alena lifted her chin. "Otherwise, you wouldn't have been on our radar."

"Only because I'm Elizabeth's roommate," Carol said. "And I was dumb enough to fall for the wrong guy."

Hank didn't believe Carol hadn't seen evidence of wrongdoing. She'd just ignored it. Like with his wife. He'd been deployed, not watching for evidence she was cheating on him.

Alena stood to pace the hotel room. "You said you know her whereabouts, and you have access to her phone. I don't think your lawyer's going to be able to argue you are unaware of what this crew are doing."

Carol stared at the FBI agent. "What do you want me to get her to say?"

Alena said, "How long will she be at the party?"

Carol glanced at her smartwatch. "At least another hour or two, I think. That's what she said to me."

Hank figured that was plenty of time for them to set up.

"Great," Alena said. "You can be in the room waiting for her when she shows up, but we'll have to be out of sight or one of the guys could spot us." Alena crossed to retrieve her laptop from the dresser, the gown swishing around her legs as she walked. She really did look beautiful— but that wasn't what Hank needed to focus on.

He checked with the plainclothes officer via text and confirmed Brittany was still downstairs at the gala event.

Alena lifted the lid of the laptop, settling back on the end of the bed. "You're scared, right?"

Carol nodded.

"Good. Use that." Alena tapped a few keys. "We need her to tell you about the business like she's trying to reassure you that everything's fine. So get her talking, tell her you're scared and maybe even thinking about quitting, if that's what it takes."

She set up the Bluetooth connection to Carol's phone, showing Hank how to do it at the same time. She had software on her laptop that she used to make the connection and transmit everything back to a program she had running. One that recorded the exchange as text.

"I'll walk you to your room, and you can rest for a bit." Alena stood. "I can give you my cell number. Text me when Brittany shows up."

Carol nodded again, not quite looking convinced. But what choice did she have?

Since Hank didn't want to remain in Alena's room alone, he said, "I'll walk her back to her suite. You get set up here."

He figured Alena wouldn't object to the chance to change her clothes. Carol didn't say much as he went with her up the elevator, to the suite she shared with the woman registered as Brittany.

"Any questions for me?" He didn't want to get into a drawn-out conversation, but if she had any fears he could allay right now, it would be a good thing.

Carol shrugged one shoulder. "I don't have much choice, do I?"

"Whether or not that's true for the feds, I would still like you to make a statement to the police department I work for so that your attack is put officially on record. That way when we find the guy who did that to you—" he motioned to the redness on Carol's neck "—we'll be able to charge him. He won't get away with it, the way people like him seem to always get away with things."

He'd noticed a lot of people felt like that. As though the world was being swallowed by a tide of evil. Hank chose to focus on the good he did every day. Rescuing people. Saving people. Helping people on the way to making their lives better after something bad or tragic had happened. Even those who had committed crimes deserved compassion and the chance to make amends—whether that meant serving a sentence before they got the opportunity to turn their lives around as a free person, or not.

Carol nodded. "I can't believe I fell for Matthew's charm. They won't let me go."

Hank wondered if she'd tried to run. "Help us find out just how far that extends. So no one else gets hurt."

She stepped into the suite and Hank headed back to Alena's room, where he knocked on the door. Inside, he heard Dax bark. How the dog knew it was him just from a knock, Hank had no idea.

She opened the door to him, wearing jeans, a T-shirt and a hoodie. "You did a good job reassuring her."

"You were listening?" He let the door shut behind him.

Alena motioned to the laptop with a wave of her hand. "I didn't turn it off. I think I'll just turn it down for a while. In case she calls anyone, or Elizabeth comes back early."

She clicked the mouse but the audio feed on the screen remained in a single line. The timer clicked to indicate recording was in progress. A small sound on Carol's end of the feed bumped the meter up and then down, creating a ripple on the line almost like a heartbeat monitor reading.

"Do you think she'll stick it out until Elizabeth gets back?"

Hank glanced over to check on Dax, but he was back against the wall, sound asleep again. "It's hard to say. There's a lot of ways this could end up gaining you nothing for your case. Is this something you do a lot?"

"Get someone to go in and gain us the information we need?" She shrugged. "It seems to be a popular tactic. A lot of agents lean more toward the result being more important than the potentially innocent person who could get caught in the crossfire."

"And where do you stand?" Hank eased into the chair at the desk where Carol had sat, still able to see the computer screen. The feed wasn't one straight line but dipped and rose sharply. "Something happening there?"

Alena strode to the laptop. "She could be taking a shower, for all we know."

Hank figured that likely wasn't what was going on. "You still need to answer my question on where you stand."

"I don't think my case is more important than a person's future." Alena toggled the volume back up.

Through the computer speakers, Carol screamed.

EIGHT

Alena raced down the hallway toward the suite, aware of Hank right on her heels. The manager's ride up the elevator to bring them a key had taken far too long, considering there was a woman in trouble. They'd joined him the rest of the ride, and when the elevator doors opened she'd silently taken the master key card and run as fast as she could down the hall.

Dax pawed at the heavy suite door, managed to tug the handle down but couldn't push it open. Hank used the key and let them in. "Dax, find."

She wasn't sure if she hoped whoever had come in and scared Carol—or worse—was still in there. Or if she hoped for their sake they were long gone. Dax made a fearsome sight racing through the room. Intent on his job.

The expansive suite had a full living room setup. Dax rounded a couch that lay on its back, spilling Carol onto the floor so that she lay across the hardwood and the back of the sofa. He sat and barked.

"Good boy, Dax." Hank slowed to kneel beside Carol.

Blood covered her chest and stomach, pooling onto the floor. Alena didn't stop. She raced to the bathroom, grabbed a handful of towels and ran back to the injured woman. If she was alive, there was no time to waste.

Hank pressed two fingers to her neck. "Heartbeat is faint, but it's there."

Alena pressed a towel to Carol's front and stacked her hands on top of each other, her elbows locked. She pressed with all her strength, putting pressure on the bleeding wounds. Just because she'd asked Carol to wear a wire didn't mean she'd invited someone to hurt the woman out of revenge. But there was still the reality of what'd happened.

Brittany was still downstairs, so who had done this?

Hank called for an ambulance from his cell phone. She hardly heard but a few snatches of the words, all her focus on the woman below her. The slight intake of breath as her body fought to keep going.

Alena stared at Carol's pale face.

"Three minutes."

She looked up at him. "Let's pray she lasts

that long." Everything in her focused on the injured woman. Alena's relationship with God hadn't been great lately. She'd had so many things go wrong the last few years, it had been hard to be honest about her anger and easier just to keep the Lord at arm's length rather than face her need to ask for help.

"This wasn't your fault."

"Of course it was." Alena gasped. Dax came over to her and licked her face. "I should have figured out how to get a camera in there, not just a listening device."

"You couldn't have known this was going to happen."

Alena shooed Dax away with a wave, not letting up pressure on Carol's wounds. Kitty, the Chihuahua, whimpered from a spot by the sofa. "Can you get her and lock her in the bathroom? Don't want her traipsing through evidence, and she'll be safe." She nodded toward the tiny dog.

Hank clicked his fingers. "Come on, Kitty."

Alena let out a breath while his back was turned. She could barely face his attention on her. Who else's fault could this disaster be? She was the one who'd persuaded Carol to help them. She'd turned this woman from a victim into an accomplice of the police—something a lot of bad guys would kill over if they discovered it happening under their noses. No one wanted to be betrayed. If it happened to a person with few inhibitions, the outcome was almost always worse.

Hank said the man who'd attacked her in the hall had driven off. Was there someone else still in the hotel? The other man, perhaps. Matthew and his friend. Two people made sense—one to kidnap Elizabeth, one to shoot at Alena.

Hank came back over. "You know something about what she went through, don't you?"

The question caught her out of nowhere.

Alena shook her head. "I have no idea what you're talking about." All she could think about was Carol, bleeding out because someone had stabbed her multiple times. A person determined not to let her get away with betraying them to the police. Alena sniffed. "Carol is dying."

"We can talk about it later." Hank squeezed her shoulder. "The EMTs are here."

Alena didn't plan on talking about it at all. She would be busy solving this case.

The door hit the wall behind it. Two men walked in, dark pants and heavy jackets with emblems, and ball caps. Giant red duffel bags and a gurney they pushed into the room.

Alena didn't let go, the towel under her hands now soaked with Carol's blood.

"Let me see." The EMT eased her aside.

Alena got out of the way so fast, she tumbled onto her behind, breathing hard, her blood pumping with adrenaline.

Hank grasped her arms and hauled her to her feet. His face swam in front of hers. "Focus on me." He paused. "Okay, take a breath. Give yourself a minute."

She shook her head. "I don't need a minute. This shouldn't have happened."

"No tragedy ever should. But we still live with it every day, and we survive because we don't have another choice."

She studied his intent gaze, desperate for that surety. Once again, she was back to doubting herself. She should call her ASAC to send other agents here to take over. She would go back to the office and let them handle it. Let Hank return to his life.

Alena had enough issues of her own without being a target, putting people's lives in danger and being the kind of agent who failed to see the truth far too often.

"Let's get her on the gurney." The EMTs both shifted and she realized she didn't know who had spoken.

Gauze and bandages now covered Carol's injuries. They lifted her onto the gurney and, seconds later, were out the door.

Alena stumbled back a step. Hank caught her arms.

"Easy."

She wanted to shake off his hold, reject the strength he seemed determined to pass to her. As a special agent, she wasn't supposed to need someone else to hold her up. The daughter her father believed he had raised should have been strong enough to weather anything, given the way he had put her through drills. Trained her in self-defense. Taught her to shoot. How to read a room.

Maybe she was those things. But in the heat of the moment, every time, she seemed to be nothing but the spinning top, swirling on the ground with no destination in mind. No ability to grasp a thought when she should have found herself with clarity of focus.

Whatever he'd tried to do with her, it seemed like he'd failed. And that wasn't the legacy she wanted her father to leave behind when he'd had such a successful career.

Maybe everyone battled self-doubt the way she did. But how did she know?

She straightened, determined not to need help.

"I'll call my chief." Hank waited until she was steady, then let go and clicked his fingers for

Dax. "We need to get evidence collection here. In case he left something behind."

Alena lifted her chin. "I already have something he left behind. An audio file of an attempted murder."

She prayed it was only "attempted" and that Carol wouldn't succumb to her injuries. Praying that might be futile. Life had taught her not to trust what she didn't fully know. That same voice whispered in her ear that she shouldn't rely on a God who seemed so distant.

She didn't want to wrestle with Him, or herself. She wanted to be certain she could do this.

Hank nodded. "Between the recording and talking to Brittany and seeing if the hotel has any kind of surveillance they wouldn't admit to before, we might actually get something."

She looked around for a murder weapon. "The manager told us they didn't have any surveillance, right?"

"I'm hoping this might change his mind into actually letting us know what they have. I know they claim they are all about their guests' privacy, but I'm just not convinced they don't have any kind of security."

Alena nodded. "Okay." This was good. She was putting her thoughts in order and coming back to herself. They had a plan now. "We should get Brittany up here. Assuming she's not somewhere, covered in Carol's blood and holding a knife."

They could have put pressure on Elizabeth before now, but her need to catch the whole crew had outweighed that. Alena needed intel on what their plan was for this weekend. She needed Elizabeth to explain why she was impersonating Brittany, a dead woman.

If they jumped now and brought Elizabeth in, the two men involved would likely split town and the FBI would never find them.

Hank tipped his head to the side. "The officer downstairs said she hasn't moved."

They'd opted to keep an officer watching "Brittany," not believing Carol was in danger, since Carol's assailant drove away earlier.

Alena winced. *How did this happen?*

"Right." Alena nodded. "Let's go get the manager first." She headed for the door and found Bremerton in the hallway still. Maybe he hadn't gone back downstairs at all.

"I had the EMTs take the service elevator." The older man frowned, worry on his face. "I don't want anyone downstairs to know what happened."

Alena wasn't sure *he* knew what had happened, or he might be less inclined to hide it. "I need you to tell me truthfully if you have any kind of surveillance on this floor, whether

in the hallway or the rooms themselves. Someone's life hangs in the balance."

They'd believed they had this covered, keeping the one uniformed officer the chief had been
able to spare downstairs keeping an eye on Brittany.

Alena had believed her plan was sound. Now
a woman's life hung in the balance.

Hank came to stand beside her. She didn't
miss the sense of solidarity they gave her, this
police officer and his K-9 partner. In the heat
of the moment, when she'd crumbled in a way
she didn't like at all, he had been there holding her up physically and emotionally. But she
couldn't get used to it.

Maybe it was the state of her career and the
disaster her love life had been. Maybe it was everything up until this point. Her father. It might
just be her being here this weekend, knowing
how much she had waiting for her at home.

All of it had brought her low at the sight of
a woman gasping for breath and bleeding out,
because Alena had put her in this situation.

Hank said, "You can't possibly tell us—"

"Okay, fine." The manager rocked back and
forth on his heels. "Let's go to the security office and we'll see what we've got."

Alena glanced at Hank, who didn't seem any

more impressed right now than she was with this guy.

A uniformed police officer showed up to take over the crime scene and they left, riding the elevator to the basement level.

The resort manager muttered something about his business teeming with cops, but Alena didn't much care about his overexaggeration. She still had to rule out his being involved.

Hank did something on his phone, sending an email by the look of what she caught over his shoulder. Probably updating his chief, which was a good idea considering a crime scene now had to be processed.

The manager let them into the security office, where an older man with white hair and the air of a corrections officer—retired—sat in a rolling office chair. "You need something, Nate?"

"Yes, thank you," Bremerton said. "Can you show us the feed for floor four?" He glanced at Hank. "How long ago?"

He looked at his watch.

Alena said, "Twelve minutes." She'd already looked at her watch in the elevator and thought through how long it had been since they'd run upstairs. "Thanks."

How long it had been since she realized she'd failed so badly.

Lord, don't let this all fall apart.

* * *

The older security guard pecked at the keyboard with two fingers but brought up the feed quickly, pressing Play so they could watch the empty hallway.

Hank glanced at Alena, trying to figure out if she was doing better or if it was only because other people were around and she had to act like the FBI special agent she was. He didn't know which. He didn't blame her reaction, given the last twenty-four hours. She'd been through plenty and was still pushing forward like a champ determined to work the case.

She hadn't been okay right after Carol was whisked off by those two EMTs. Then again, he hadn't been okay either. Hank just let the emotion out differently than she did. Neither was bad, simply a product of who they were and what they needed to do to bleed off the stresses of their jobs.

However, what Alena held below the surface had peeked through a couple of times. Enough that he wondered what she kept private and if she would trust him—as a friend, of course—and share with him. He wondered if the parts of him he didn't share got out like that and if she wanted to know more.

If she was at all to blame for what'd happened down the hall, then he was also.

Both of them had to trust that they'd done everything they could to help Carol out of a bad situation. They would have argued to the DA that she go free, or face drastically reduced charges, in exchange for the help she'd given them today. Instead, all they'd been able to do was have the EMTs dispatched as fast as possible after the worst happened.

Neither could have predicted someone would enter the room and try to kill Carol.

Had it been Matthew or someone else? There were still far too many unanswered questions.

A minute or so later, a man strode down the hall. Dark jeans and a dark hoodie, boots on his feet. The feed was black-and-white and grainy. Under the hood he'd pulled over his head, Hank could see the bill of a ball cap when he turned his head very slightly.

A man trying to do his utmost to disguise his features for any hidden cameras. Yet, Hank noted, not overtly keeping his identity under wraps by wearing a full face mask.

"No way to identify him." Hank tried to sigh out the frustration. "Maybe when he comes out though."

The man entered the hotel room using a key card.

Alena said, "We need to know how many of those were issued for this room. And who they were given to." She paused a second. "The audio recording might give us something from inside the room."

He wasn't sure if Alena was reassuring herself or everyone else with that statement. Before he could ask, the man exited the room and walked down the hall with something in his hand.

Hank frowned. "Is that the knife he used to try to kill her?" He peered closer at the screen as the man veered to the wall and moved his arms. "What was that? What did he do?"

The manager shifted. "That's a trash chute."

Hank and Alena twisted to look at each other.

"He dumped the knife." They both said the words at the same time.

Hank turned to the manager as he followed Alena to the door. He called back, "Please make sure the police department gets that footage."

"The trash chute dumps out down the hall from here," Bremerton called out. "Left."

Hank ran to the door after Alena. He saw she had gone right. "Alena! He said left." Hank waited for her to turn, then made his way down the hall, checking each door for the trash.

The last door on the right read Storage and Disposal.

Hank pushed the handle and stepped inside. "Looks like a giant open-top trash bin." They probably wheeled it out the garage-style door on the far exterior wall.

They both moved to the edge and peered in.

Alena said, "We need gloves."

Hank turned and looked around. He found rows of storage shelves. Next to bottles of cleaning supplies, he discovered a box of extra-thick protective gloves probably meant for the custodial staff. "Here."

He handed some to her and donned a pair. She climbed in, but he could reach far enough inside to check just shifting stuff out of the way. After searching through the dumpster for fifteen minutes, Alena straightened. "Got it."

He looked up to find her holding a darkly stained knife. The grin on her face lit up her entire expression. "We found it."

Instead of looking at the weapon, he kept his attention on Alena. Like a shot of hope in a dark place. And he probably wasn't supposed to find her attractive in a dumpster surrounded by trash, holding a murder weapon, but Hank had long ago given up the rhyme or reason of why he found a woman attractive. Besides, it was far better than dwelling on the worst parts of this day.

Even in the midst of this case, he'd found himself drawn to Alena—and immediately tried to shut down those feelings. He'd made an ironclad agreement with himself that he would never fall for a woman again. He and Alena had only known each other for a couple of days. Taking that risk again just wasn't worth it.

Maybe it wasn't fair on womankind, but when his heart was on the line, he had to fall back on that old adage of rescuer safety first. He had been a first responder for several years now. His resolve just wasn't something he would give up on overnight, all because of one pretty face.

Hank had to keep himself safe before he could possibly help anyone else. That meant keeping his heart intact and not getting himself in situations where it would be broken all over again.

Another uniformed officer showed up, called there by Hank's email to his boss. He deposited the knife into the evidence bag the officer had brought with him. "Get that back to the station. It needs to be processed and tested."

Yet another piece of evidence they weren't likely to find fingerprints on anytime soon—the lab would take too long. But that wasn't going to be how they solved this case.

"We need to show that footage to Brittany and see if she has any idea who might have tried to kill Carol." He glanced over at Alena.

"First, we need to see if she's already aware it happened." Alena lifted her chin, none of her earlier shock registering on her face. "If she knows Carol, has she heard about the stabbing?"

He nodded, a surge of respect rising in him. "Good. Let's go."

She found the restroom on the ground floor and washed up while he stood at the entry to the gala and scanned the crowd, keeping an eye on Brittany. The young woman wandered around the room, talking and laughing. Drinking from the slender glass she held in two fingers. If she cared at all about Carol, it was apparent that she didn't know her roommate had been attacked. Or, at least, the hotel's hush-hush policy meant word hadn't gotten down to the gala.

Or she didn't care at all. Kind of like how she didn't seem to care she'd been kidnapped yesterday and spent half the night in the hospital.

"I'll wait here." Alena emerged from the restroom and came over to his side.

He had to admit she didn't fit in the gala any longer, wearing her jeans and a hoodie. His suit might be rumpled and speckled with blood, but if he moved quickly, no one would notice. Dax always drew more attention than Hank did anyway.

He patted the dog's head and walked swiftly to Brittany's side. "Ms. Hattenden?" As if that was her real name. "If you'd come with me for a moment?" He spoke low so no one nearby heard them.

It was probably the only reason why she walked with him.

"Right this way." He wasn't going to engage with her. As far as he was concerned, she was a suspect. Only, was that because of Alena's impression of her or had the night's events put her even further under suspicion?

The whole thing was a delicate balance. But if he stuck to procedure and did what he should, they would come up with even more evidence. The police department here would solve this crime with the FBI's help—and he would be in the middle of it the way he wanted.

He stepped into the hall and looked around. The hallway was empty, but none of the patrons back in the gala was the person he was looking for anyway.

"What did you want to talk to me about?"

He turned to Brittany and she slid her hands up his chest. Interest flared in her eyes.

Hank took a step back.

He turned in a circle again. "Where did Alena go?"

NINE

The man's grip on her arm pinged the nerve from Alena's elbow down to her hand where her fingers tingled. Bile rose in her throat. He shoved her ahead of him down the hallway, out of sight of anyone.

And if she screamed?

He would shoot an innocent person.

She gritted her teeth and didn't make a sound. Of *course* she hadn't grabbed her gun from the room before she and Hank had run upstairs to Carol. She twisted and tried to see his face but he held on to her too tightly that she couldn't turn far enough to see with him so close to her.

She'd figured it was a smart move to stick in the hallway in her casual clothes and wait for Hank to bring the young woman out so they could question her about who would try to kill her roommate. And why.

Now she didn't think that had been such a good idea.

He pushed over her shoulder on the door marked Stairs and shoved her into a concrete stairwell. He'd walked up behind her in the hall outside the gala and stuck this gun in her ribs. The same one that jabbed her now. Then he'd grabbed her arm and she'd swallowed the need to cry out.

His hot breath had washed against her ear, explaining she'd better not make a sound. She should come with him, or he would start shooting innocent bystanders. She'd heard that loud and clear with his rank breath on her cheek.

Alena spun back again to try and get a look at him. "Hello, Matthew." This was the man who had shoved Carol up against the wall.

The man who had stabbed Carol—or so she figured—now had a gun. He wore similar clothing to the man from the surveillance footage, but no hoodie. He had a jacket, where he'd worn a suit earlier this evening. Just a short time ago, before he'd fled. He had to have changed somewhere close by. Maybe this Matthew person was a different guy than the one who'd stabbed Carol. The fourth person in their group.

His face was fully visible—dark brown eyes, thick brows and that tiny scar on his neck—which didn't bode well. He wasn't worried she would identify him later and he wasn't trying to hide his identity.

Because she wouldn't be alive to tell anyone what he looked like?

He raised the gun to point it right at her face. "Get moving."

She had no opening to fight him hand to hand. There were moves for disarming a gunman when she had no weapon, but maybe he knew them because his body was angled slightly. She wouldn't be able to do much before he either hit her on the head with that pistol or shot her. *Not good.*

Alena turned and trod slowly down the stairs. Her sneakers made no sound, whereas his boots pounded the steps behind her. That meant he was heavier than he looked. She'd ascertained he was knowledgeable about self-defense and fighting skills. He knew what he was doing with that gun.

"Are you the one who kidnapped Brittany right in front of me?" She kept moving, prepared in case he tried to shove her. "Or the one who stabbed Carol earlier?" She grabbed the rail and held on as she continued down. "Or both."

No sense falling if she didn't have to. Then again, he was likely going to kill her either way.

Once she was out of the way of civilians, she needed to get the jump on him.

Given she hadn't seen the man who'd kidnapped Brittany, because of the ski mask, or who had stabbed Carol, thanks to the security footage, she had no idea what he'd done. The only thing she could definitely ID him for was accosting Carol.

Either way, he would be under arrest.

Did Hank know where they'd gone? He would come after her, and Dax would find her. No matter where this guy took her, they would find her.

She rounded the next landing, which led to the rear parking garage where the valet stored cars and to the bay for deliveries. "Where are we going?"

"Shut up and keep walking." He jabbed the gun into her back hard enough it would be bruised tomorrow.

It wasn't morbid to contemplate what evidence he'd leave behind on her for the medical examiner. Her dad had taught her to be realistic and think about things rationally. Death was a part of life, and with her job she had seen people whose lives had been taken in the worst ways. Victims.

She'd never thought that one day it might be her.

Alena gritted her teeth. He likely had a car waiting. Maybe he couldn't have known he'd find her in the hallway outside the gala, but it seemed like he wasn't reacting. More like this was a plan. Or this split-second decision to kidnap her hadn't spiked his emotions. At least, not enough she might be able to catch him off guard and turn the tables.

She needed a strategy that would give her a shot at getting out of here.

Alena blew out a slow breath, trying to ease the pounding of her heart. "So I can't ask why you're kidnapping me, then?" The plan involved letting him think she was scared, as any victim would be.

"You're a cop. I don't like cops." Jab. "That's enough."

She bit back the need to ask what he intended to do to her. Alena stopped in front of the door to the lower level: the resort laundry and storage for the chairs and things they set out for events. The same place they'd found the murder weapon.

"Open the door."

Alena pushed it wide and found it too heavy to slam back in his face before he could move through it. The door would keep a fire contained, but it moved far too slowly across the floor to be useful when she needed it to keep a gunman from shooting her.

She shuffled forward, keeping her body language firmly set to *scared out of my mind.*

"Maybe you should tell me who you really are before you kill me, *Matthew*?"

He chuckled. "You ask too many questions, but that's not surprising. You stick your nose into things you should leave alone."

She scanned the hallway ahead of her. She spotted a housekeeping cart but throwing towels at him wouldn't help. A mop bucket on one end. Could she draw out the handle and manage to hit him before he shot her?

He shoved her back.

Alena stumbled. She grasped the cart, twisted her hips and snatched a jug of bleach from the top of the cart. She swung it around, sideswiping his gun arm. The gun discharged with a flash of light and a deafening boom. She slammed the jug into his head while her ears rang.

Alena dropped the jug. He grabbed for her, but she shoved him and took off down the hall.

The gun went off again, missing her. *Thank You, Lord.*

She ducked to the side and slammed against a door. Alena grabbed the handle and twisted it, rushing inside as another gunshot pinged off the doorframe. She slammed it shut and locked it.

He banged on the door.

Every breath could be her last.

She had to get out of there fast. Keep moving, find an escape in this maze of hallways.

Alena turned into the room and found rows of huge laundry machines with a door at the end. She ran toward it.

Through it.

Another room, this one with stacks of sheets and towels. Huge ironing machines hovered over plates, machines whirring around her.

The door in the washing room splintered.

Alena ran for somewhere to hide.

The resort manager used his master key card to let Hank into Alena's room. Explaining the situation to Bremerton had taken far too much time, but if Hank wanted to find her, he needed Dax.

"Thank you." Hank pushed the door open and let his K-9 partner in first.

"I'll check with security and see if we can't figure out what happened."

"Yep." Hank barely acknowledged the guy. "Ready to work, Dax?" He used an excited tone the dog understood more than the words themselves, which weren't a command. "Let's get a scent."

He found the shirt Alena had worn yesterday on the floor beside her suitcase, then the leash he'd taken off Dax on the dresser. They'd run out so fast, he hadn't grabbed it.

Hank pushed out a breath in the elevator. He

tried to get rid of the frantic feeling making his hands shake and his heart pound in his chest. He might not have known Alena for long, but he didn't like to lose anyone.

Someone had taken her.

Every instinct he had said she hadn't gone off on her own or left of her own free will. After how she'd been in shock following Carol being stabbed, there was no way she'd have let herself be that vulnerable—even for the chance to solve a case.

If anyone could find her, it was Dax.

Looking at the surveillance footage would take too long. His partner was much faster.

Down in the hallway outside the gala, Hank held out the shirt for Dax and said, "Get it." When he had the scent, Hank said, "Seek."

Dax turned around, sniffing the floor in the spot Hank had left Alena standing.

A prayer whispered from his lips even though it had been a long time since he'd prayed for anything personal. Usually his prayers were reserved for the people he was trying to find, and for helping him get to them fast—which was mostly down to Dax.

His dog caught the scent among so many and raced down the hall. Hank jogged to keep pace with him.

He lifted a hand, tugged at his tie and managed to get his collar button unfastened. Hank heaved a breath. *Much better.*

Dax rounded the corner and headed down a less-used hallway. He slowed at the door marked Stairs and sniffed at the base, in a line left to right.

"Okay." Hank pulled down the handle.

Dax knew not to dart through, even in pursuit of a scent.

Hank glanced around to clear the small concrete landing, then said, "Seek."

Dax headed down. They rounded each floor until he reached the lowest level, one floor below the parking garage. Hank cracked the door, held it with his foot and pulled out his weapon from the shoulder holster under his jacket.

He pushed the door wider. "Seek."

Dax headed along the hall, through the maze of what looked like storage and maintenance rooms. A cart up against the wall. A bottle of bleach lying on the floor a couple feet away— a dent in the bottom. Dax slowed to sniff at the handle.

A man wearing coveralls rounded the corner at the end.

Hank brought up his weapon and the man's eyes widened. "Whoa."

He shifted his gun away. The guy had a name

tag, a tool belt and a radio. His bald head shone from the overhead light. Hank said, "Have you seen a woman down here?"

The guy shook his head. "You looking for one in particular?"

Hank indicated Dax, wearing his Search and Rescue vest. "He is. Do me a favor?"

The guy shrugged.

"Call the manager. Ask if he found anything from the surveillance."

"Ain't no surveillance down here. So if the woman you're looking for came this way, it won't be on the security footage." The man sniffed.

"Ask anyway. And I have another question."

The guy shrugged. "Shoot."

"Have you seen a man down here in the last fifteen minutes?"

"Maybe. Heard footsteps a bit ago. Someone ran off."

"Thanks." Hank said, "Dax, Seek."

The dog went to a door and they wandered through a laundry room. The maintenance guy followed, calling for the manager on his radio. Asking if security knew anything about a missing woman.

The security guard responded, "Yeah, the boss's here now. We called the PD, 'cause it looks like some guy forced her into the stairwell."

Hank's chest felt like it had steel bands around it. He sucked in a breath, wanting to tell Dax to hurry even though it didn't work like that and his dog would only get confused. That would slow him down, at a time when he wanted nothing to keep Dax from finding Alena.

The K-9 headed for an interior door.

They moved into a room that looked like a place where they ironed sheets en masse. He couldn't hold back, muttering, "Come on, Alena. Where are you?"

Why would she come into a room like this with no exit? Had her assailant forced her in here at gunpoint and then forced her to… *No.* He couldn't let his mind go there. If he did, he would be paralyzed by fear. His dog could give him some kind of slight signal and he'd miss it, too caught up in his fear for a woman he had to admit he cared about. Probably more than he should.

Where are you, Alena?

Dax put on a burst of speed and headed for a stack of dirty sheets piled almost to his waist. His K-9 partner sat.

Okay, then. "Good boy. Good boy." Hank rubbed the sides of Dax's face then turned to the pile. He dropped the leash and pulled away handfuls of sheets.

Alena gasped and launched up.

"Whoa." He caught her in his arms. "Whoa, it's okay. I've got you."

Her breath came in heaves. Dax barked. Hank hung on to her. "You good?"

She nodded, trembling in his arms. He understood the strength she had—and now he understood the depth of feeling vulnerable and powerless. He'd experienced both as a marine, facing down the enemy. Now he knew she understood it, too.

Their cheeks brushed. Sensation rose in him, the attraction that wanted to override all his logic and good reasoning. Hank pushed it down in favor of something professional. He stepped back slightly from the reflex to pull her close. He kept that hold on her arms, just so she didn't fall to the floor.

"You were hiding?" He cleared his throat. "From him?"

She nodded again. No longer cheek to cheek, he could see the glaze in her eyes. "It sounded like he ran off."

Hank recalled what the maintenance guy had said about seeing a man leave. "I think he may have gotten spooked and left." The alternative wasn't something he could think about. They would find him, through the surveillance. Following procedure. They *would* get this guy.

"He forced me down here at gunpoint." She

let go of her hold on his jacket to brush hair back from her face. "He was going to kill me."

Hank nodded, trying to tamp down his reaction to realizing she was gone from that hall. "I'm glad you're all right."

"We need to find him and arrest him."

"Did you see his face?"

She lifted her chin. "Yes, I did. It was Matthew."

TEN

"If you can walk, the EMTs can meet us in the lobby."

Alena nodded. "Lobby, yes. Medics, no. I don't need to see a doctor. I'm fine."

Maybe that wasn't completely true, but it also wasn't a lie. She was all right even if what had just happened had seriously shaken her. As long as no one else was hurt, and no one had been killed, what did it matter?

They headed for the elevator. Hank stopped to talk to an older man in overalls. He seemed interested in her, but Alena didn't want to talk to anyone so she leaned against the wall and waited for the door to slide open. Dax came over to her, sniffing her shoe before he turned and sat with his back to her. She didn't know what that meant but it was comforting with him in a kind of guard position.

Hank shook the guy's hand and came over.

"He didn't see Matthew's face. Just his back as he ran away like a coward." His nose scrunched up.

"That might not be exactly what happened." She almost wanted to laugh, he looked so mad. Had anyone ever been that angry on her behalf? Her father, maybe. That thought brought with it a wave of sadness encompassing everything she'd lost in the last few months. *Oh, Dad.*

"What is it?"

Before she could figure out how to brush off his question so she didn't have to talk about her father, the elevator doors opened. Alena stepped in. Dax followed her, and Hank leaned against the wall. "Answer the question, Alena."

She looked at the doors as the elevator did that lurch they all did and started to rise. "I was just thinking about something, and it doesn't have anything to do with the case."

He didn't look satisfied. "Fine. So why'd he run off?"

"Matthew?"

Hank nodded. "You hid, and he abandoned searching for you?"

"He was going to kill me." Alena blew out a breath. She needed to acknowledge the threat so she could process the fading adrenaline and everything else that came with it. Not just the physical symptoms of what had happened, but the mental and emotional. She'd sat with enough victims to know the effects would linger for a time.

She pulled in a lungful of air and blew that out slowly, a fresh, cleansing breath. "He brought me down here to kill me. Probably because it was easier to get rid of the FBI agent than avoid me. He had a gun, and I knew it was better to get him away from innocent people, so I went with him."

"You let him bring you down to the basement?"

"He knew where he was going, but I grabbed that bleach jug and hit him with it. I ran."

"Good."

The hard tone of his voice made her feel better, though she wasn't going to admit that to him or anyone else. The elevator doors slid open but she didn't step out right away. Hank led Dax by his leash and motioned with his head for her to follow.

They stepped out into the busy lobby.

"We need to talk to Brittany. Or whatever her name is." Alena looked around for her and spotted a uniformed police officer.

Hank frowned at her but headed for the guy without saying anything.

She really didn't want to see an EMT, nor did she need one. She wasn't injured, and all she'd done was hide under a pile of dirty sheets. She probably looked as good as that pile had.

Alena shoved her hands in her pockets and her fingers touched a hair tie in the right pocket. *Thank You.* She had no problem giving God credit for that foresight. Some people might think it strange to thank the Lord for something so simple, but she'd found Him more in the everyday mundane things than in huge works of His that seemed so unlikely.

She tugged her hair into a ponytail, which made her feel much better. She found a sore spot on the back of her head that explained the headache. She must have banged her head, but like her knee from when Brittany had been kidnapped, it wasn't bad.

Hank spoke with the officer, a guy with "Stephans" on his name badge. She stopped beside Hank and caught the tail end of him asking about Brittany.

"She's still talking to the same man." The officer pointed into the busy gala room then looked at Alena. "Glad you're all right."

She nodded. "Thanks."

"You can ID the guy?"

She said, "Sure can. And we need to talk to Brittany. Find out who he is."

Carol was out of commission. Alena didn't even know if she'd survived so far, but figured she was probably in surgery. When she woke up—if she pulled through the stabbing attack—they could talk to her. It could be days before they got the chance though.

"Brittany" was their shot at information. Alena didn't want to feel the regret of not pressing the woman more in the hospital. But if she'd tried hard to talk to Elizabeth before all of this had happened tonight, Carol might not have been injured.

"I'll get her for you." The officer strode into the room. He had his uniform on, so it would be more official than Hank in his suit or her in her jeans and hoodie.

Alena needed her badge, but she'd come here undercover and hadn't wanted anyone to see it and reveal her true identity. She'd tucked it in her suitcase when she'd changed for the gala and hadn't grabbed it before Carol was stabbed.

Hank glanced at her.

"I'm fine."

He snorted. "You just need a nap, the chance to freshen up and three cups of coffee."

Alena grinned. "Exactly."

"Are you going to be able to sleep tonight in your hotel room?"

Probably not. "I don't have much choice, do I?" She needed rest.

Before he could say anything, the officer

came out. Brittany blustered, starting to argue—probably against the officer and the grip he had on her arm.

Officer Stephans said, "Don't start with me. You think that man was fooled by your act? Please."

Alena got the impression someone had broken his heart, but now wasn't the time to get into that. "Ms. Hattenden? We know that's not your real name, but we need to speak to you."

Brittany tugged her arm from the officer's grasp. "I don't have to say anything."

"True." Alena folded her arms. "You can choose to say nothing. Meanwhile I'll talk to the US attorney and you'll be facing murder charges, accessory to attempted murder, theft and entrapment charges. Along with anything else I can come up with."

"I'm the victim here." She practically stomped her foot. "I was kidnapped yesterday!"

Alena wanted to argue that if that were the case, Dax probably wouldn't have his ears back while he sniffed the woman. "And the police here still need your statement about that. So let's find somewhere quiet to talk." She took a step back and waved to a conference room across the hall.

Officer Stephans said, "I'll go find the manager and look at security. See if we can't find an image of that coward running away after he realized it was too difficult to kill you."

Hank coughed—it sounded like he was covering a laugh.

Alena wasn't so amused, but she appreciated his attempt at making her feel better. "Thank you, Officer Stephans." She turned to the woman. "Brittany?"

Maybe she should use the name Elizabeth.

Hank said, "We're going to need to see your real ID. Then you can tell us about Matthew, and everything else."

Alena hadn't had a partner in a while but had to admit it didn't feel bad knowing she had cops around her. Watching her back.

Not to mention a K-9 who had found her hiding place and rescued her.

She was going to buy Dax the biggest treat she could find. Then she would go home and tell her dad all about the hero dog and his marine partner.

"This way, ma'am." Hank led Brittany to the conference room.

Soon enough, Alena would leave this town and go back to Wyoming. Back to her life.

Why did that thought make her sad?

Hank had Brittany take a seat. Alena shut the door, and Hank told Dax to lie down. He needed to get his good boy a treat. Dax had found Alena in the basement under that pile of sheets. The alternative wasn't something he could even think about.

Matthew had been there to kill Alena.

Whatever had caused him to break away and run, whether it was not finding her hiding spot or being drawn away by someone or something else, Hank wanted to fall to his knees and thank God it had worked out like that. If not for Dax, he could still be looking for her.

If not for God's hand on it, he could've found her after it was too late.

He turned a chair to face Brittany and sat. "Do you have identification with your real name?"

Her face had blanked, her expression placid in a way he didn't believe at all. She just hadn't figured out how to play this yet.

Alena folded her arms and leaned against the wall. The woman looked exhausted—but then, he was, too. They could both use some rest, and it was late. After they wrapped this up, he was going to get her to sleep for a while. Let the Sundown Valley PD work this case overnight.

Brittany sighed. She unzipped the clutch purse she'd tossed on the table when she'd sat. "Fine."

She slid a driver's license across the table. Texas, and it was expired.

Hank read the name. "So Elizabeth Cunningham is who you really are?" He'd wondered, since they knew for sure she wasn't Brittany. "Nice to meet you."

"Whatever." She rolled her eyes. "I just didn't want to die and be a Jane Doe someone found."

Alena spoke up from her spot by the door. "Like the real Brittany Hattenden. The woman you murdered so you could take her place here."

Elizabeth twisted around in her chair. "I didn't kill her!"

"That doesn't mean you're not an accessory to her death," Alena said. "Whoever shot her, you know what they did."

Hank figured she planned to convince this woman to testify against Matthew and the other man involved.

"They tried to do the same to Carol." Alena let that statement hang in the air.

Elizabeth's eyes flashed. "What?"

"In your room." Hank tried to figure out how long ago that had been. A couple of hours? For some reason, it felt like a lot longer. "Earlier this evening. She's in critical condition at the hospital. Fighting for her life because she got sucked into this thing with you and Matthew, and whoever else you're working with."

Elizabeth shifted in her seat.

"Tell me who abducted you."

She lifted her gaze to him, tears in her eyes he didn't believe. "It was Matthew. He wouldn't let me go. He said he needed to teach me a lesson."

"But he left you alive." And now she carried her ID in case anyone found her dead body.

Elizabeth sniffed. "You guys are the ones who found me. So you know what happened. I didn't ask for it, like I didn't ask for any of this. My boyfriend..." She cleared her throat.

Hank glanced at Alena, just to see how she felt about what Elizabeth was saying. He couldn't read the expression on her face.

"What's your boyfriend's name?"

Hank wanted to know the answer to that question as well. When Elizabeth didn't answer, he said, "You need to start being straight with us, Elizabeth. Matthew grabbed Alena. Unlike with you, he intended to kill her. Something stopped him. Meanwhile, Carol is fighting for her life."

"Where's Kitty?"

"Still in your room, though the resort staff were going to check on her and let her out. When Carol was stabbed, we put your dog in the bathroom." Her thing with her dog bordered on ridiculous considering she'd thrown the animal at Alena when she was kidnapped, but he wasn't anyone to talk about someone else's attachment to a canine. He couldn't imagine life without Dax.

Hank looked over at his partner. Chin on his paws, watching them. Keeping him safe the same way he'd watched out for Alena on their way up here. Was Dax getting sweet on the FBI agent the same way Hank was? He wouldn't be surprised.

"Phew." An expression washed over Elizabeth's face that didn't quite track with being worried about her dog. At least, not *just* that.

Hank said, "You need to tell us what's going on here. Who are these guys and how did you get tangled with them?"

Carol hadn't been in it more than a few weeks. She'd been dragged in by Matthew, who she'd said was her boyfriend. Was Elizabeth in a relationship with the other guy?

"You think I can just tell you everything?" Elizabeth glanced between them.

"They tried to kill Carol." Hank figured she couldn't argue with that. "Would you rather face them, or take your chances with us?"

"Like you're gonna give me a deal?" she scoffed.

Alena said, "Depends what you have to say. Make it worth my while, and I'll make sure you get a fair shake with the prosecutor."

When Elizabeth looked like she was going to argue, Hank said, "This offer won't last forever. You can either cooperate or make things difficult for us. We can reciprocate either way. One of those will go better for you."

Alena said, "Start talking."

"Okay, you don't need to yell at me." Elizabeth sniffed. "I'll tell you, okay? Only so I don't get stabbed like Carol, all right. My boyfriend said he would kill me if I messed this up." She whimpered. "I don't have a choice. Matthew is crazy."

"So you're together. You and Matthew?" Hank asked.

She shook her head. "No. I'm with Steve. Carol is with Matthew."

"Steve what?"

She shrugged. "He just said his name was Steve. We've only been together a few weeks."

Hank said, "Do you have a photo of him on your phone?"

"No." Elizabeth shook her head. "He said not to take a picture of him." She sniffled, but no tears fell.

Alena interjected then. "What are you all here this weekend to do?"

"It's done," Elizabeth said. "They already got the jewels, this morning while all the doctors and their wives were at the breakfast listening to their guest speaker."

Hank's stomach dropped.

Alena said, "Then why stick around if they've already taken what they were here to steal?"

Elizabeth winced. "Steve realized one of the wives had a million-dollar necklace. But it would've made it obvious we'd stolen everything if he'd taken it this morning. So he had me distract the husband tonight…while he seduced the wife and stole it."

"But they had no time to make a forgery," Alena said.

Elizabeth nodded. "He wanted the payday. He said we had to stick around and get it. That we could retire. We'd be rich."

Hank blew out a long breath. "Where are Matthew and Steve now?"

"Steve is probably still up in the wife's room." Elizabeth reached for her phone in the clutch purse. "I don't keep tabs on Matthew. I try to avoid him as much as I can."

Alena pushed off the wall. "Which room?"

Elizabeth was about to say when the door opened. Officer Stephans stuck his head in, face pale. He found Hank and said, "I called the chief. The head of security was beaten and left for dead. All the security footage has been deleted."

"Get the manager as well." Hank stood. "And sit with this woman until I come back down." To Elizabeth he said, "Which room is Steve in?"

Her lip quivered. "Three-twelve."

Alena headed out the door first. Hank said, "Dax," like his name was a command of its own.

His dog hopped up and followed, though it seemed more like he was intently following Alena. They rode the elevator upstairs. While it ascended, he said, "This thing is spiraling."

"But we're closer now than my team has ever been."

"Good," Hank said. "But that doesn't mean we're about to close the case." They had two men to find. Would one be up here, trying to steal a necklace while a woman he was supposed to care for languished in police custody? Neither man involved was the kind Hank could respect. They were nothing but deadbeats.

The kinds of criminals who needed to face justice.

When the elevator doors opened, he had Dax go first. Alena and Hank jogged after him. He whistled and indicated the room, then knocked on the door. A flustered older woman answered, hair and dress rumpled. "You got here so fast. I've been robbed!"

"Where's the thief?" Alena asked.

"He ran off!" she wailed and touched her cheeks with both hands. "He just took it and ran! I thought we had something special."

Alena turned to Hank. "Just like Matthew. He ran."

"Maybe that's why." They had what they wanted.

And now they were gone.

ELEVEN

Alena pushed back the comforter and got up, wanting to push away the fatigue so easily. But getting up was better than continuing to lie there while her thoughts spun around and around about the case and everything that'd happened. She had asked her ASAC, Brent Waterson, to call this morning. So she'd better be up.

She tugged on a sweater over her lounge pants and T-shirt and added a pair of socks since the wood floor proved cold under her bare feet.

In the end, she'd packed her suitcase and spent the night in the guest room at Hank's house— his surprisingly *adorable* ranch-style house. It hadn't taken much convincing after he'd mentioned he lived just inside town limits, with a room that he'd planned for his brother to use.

His brother hadn't taken advantage of the offer, choosing instead to live across town. Hank had explained that he had two acres, and he paid a couple of kids from the youth group at church to maintain a garden on them. Mostly potatoes. When the last thing she'd wanted to think about was what had almost happened to her in the lowest level of the resort, she'd jumped at the chance to stay away from the place. Not just because potatoes were her favorite food.

She hadn't wanted him to know exactly how shaken up she was after that man had forced her down the stairs at gunpoint, but she could tell he knew.

A storm had blown in overnight, coating the area in new snow and making travel in and out of the resort difficult. She wondered if that would end up helping them though, if their perpetrators would also be hampered because of the weather.

After a quick bathroom trip, where she found everything had been updated to modern finishings, she headed for the yummy smells coming from the kitchen.

At the sight of him standing by the stove, holding a spatula with one hand and a mug with the other, she stopped.

With her mind looking for something—anything—to think on except the fear she'd felt the night before, the complexity of this case and the rest of this disastrous weekend, she found herself soaking in this man. A former marine. A first responder. Exactly the kind of man her father would've loved to nudge her toward.

Alena tugged her phone from her sweater pocket and sent a text to the nurse, asking for an update on her father.

A wet dog nose nudged her hand.

"Hello." She looked down at Dax, petting his head. "Good morning to you."

Hank chuckled. "He was pacing the hallway this morning when I got up. Playing guard dog outside your room."

As much as she wanted to settle into something that didn't resemble work at all, she slid onto a bar stool and said, "Have there been any updates?"

"First, coffee."

Alena chuckled. "I thought safety was first."

"I'm a marine. Your dad is one. You *have* to know that safety is like…third, at best. It's always coffee first." He set a full mug in front of her. "Cream?"

She shook her head. "Black."

"Breakfast?"

"With a side of morning briefing."

Hank chuckled. "Fair enough." He went to stir whatever he had in the pan before he said, "Chief Willa emailed this morning. He's got the manager for the resort on the task of talking to their IT storage company about retrieving all the data that was deleted. Once he gets that, they'll go through surveillance and provide us with images of every male who is currently checked in, and those who've been through the common areas recently."

Alena nodded. "We need to ID Matthew. His real name. And find his partner."

She took a sip of surprisingly great coffee—she'd have to find out where he bought his beans—and found a calendar on the wall. A veterans' fundraiser calendar, which indicated it was Sunday. Not that she'd forgotten, but the reminder wasn't exactly welcome considering she was running out of time to solve this case.

She pushed out a breath.

"Still thinking about it?"

"Not that, but yes." She figured she might as well tell him what he already knew. "It won't leave my mind."

He turned off the burner under the skillet and came back over. He stood on the other side of the breakfast bar, the coffee still in his hand. "My first firefight in the marine corps, I totally freaked out. Froze up. Had to have my sergeant smack me upside the head to knock me out of it."

"It wasn't my first case."

"First time at gunpoint?"

Alena shook her head. "Is it the same every

time, or does it get easier? Because maybe it should be better by now."

"Not necessarily." He shrugged. "There's some of that tendency to freeze every time, like it's latent in me. I have to push past it and get to the core of strength I know is under there because the marine corps forged that in me."

"My dad did the same to me." She set her mug down and played with the handle. "I guess he tried anyway."

"You saw his face. You knew Matthew was there to kill you."

She nodded.

"Did you freeze up?"

"Not completely. But what else was I supposed to do but go with him. Get him away from all those bystanders. When I did that, I used what I could. Then I ran."

"You kept your head." Instead of judgment on his face, all she saw was compassion.

"It was the same guy who attacked Carol." Alena frowned. "But was it the same man who stabbed her? I can't imagine one person being that busy." She shook her head. "Does your department have a sketch artist you use?" It wasn't ideal. That would take time.

"She doesn't work Sundays. It's a rule. She's at church." He moved to retrieve two bowls from a high cupboard and distributed the food into both. "Chef's special. Sausage, potato and egg."

"You're an amazing man."

He chuckled. "If that's how easy it is to make you happy, then great."

"The potato on its own would have succeeded."

He slid onto the stool beside hers and pushed over the sauce bottle with a smile. "Good to know."

Alena took a bite. As breakfast went, it was pretty standard, but she hadn't had to make it herself so it tasted better than it would if she had. She finished a bite and cleared her throat with a sip of coffee. "It's great. Thanks."

Hank chuckled around his mouthful. When he'd swallowed, he said, "So a sketch artist image is out."

"But your chief is working with the manager to get a surveillance image. Because Elizabeth is apparently the only woman in existence who doesn't take a photo of the man she's in a relationship with. And they're not local guys."

"We'll have to pick him out like it's a photo array."

She wasn't backing down. "I can do that."

"Me, too, for the guy I chased away." He paused. "I'm still waiting for the results of that partial plate to be narrowed down, but all we have so far is a long list of possible vehicles for the department to sift through. It will probably end up being a car that was reported stolen."

"So not only do we have to ID one guy we've seen, but we also have to ID another guy only Carol and Elizabeth know."

She had wondered the same thing in the time she'd been awake last night. Evicted from her sleep by a nasty dream about a man with his arm up against her throat. The man with the gun. Matthew. Another man she didn't want to think about.

Her ex, Chadwell, had no business occupying her thoughts. Not anymore. Alena had been up close and personal with Matthew.

Too personal.

Hank frowned. "Did Matthew say anything to you?"

She looked down at her bowl, formulating her thoughts while she figured out how to answer.

"You can just tell me the truth."

She'd already given his department a statement before they'd left the resort last night. Couldn't he just read that?

"Alena, tell me what he said."

She sucked in a breath, trying to gather strength. "He said I was a meddling FBI agent who should know better than to stick her nose into things that weren't my business. That I would learn." Her voice broke on that last word, and she shivered.

"He was goading you." Hank touched her arm. "Because you're a threat to his business."

She shook her head. "I might be an FBI agent, but sometimes I don't think I'm a threat to anyone."

Hank stared at her. "How is that even possible?"

The woman thought she represented zero threat to Matthew and his associate. So then, why would they bother trying to kill her? If she meant nothing to their success, they'd have ignored her completely.

Alena groaned. He wished he could reassure her...and tell her she looked beautiful, even rumpled from hard days working a difficult case.

She pushed away her empty bowl. "I was working a case not all that dissimilar to this one. Maybe that's why I'm so set to solve it." She tugged over her mug and looked inside.

Hank took it. "I'll get you some more."

Maybe she would feel more comfortable with him on the other side of the breakfast bar, like he had been. He usually changed out of sweats and a T-shirt on Sundays and went to church. Today it wasn't worth risking bystanders if anything happened, so he'd live streamed on the TV from one of his favorite congregations. He figured he couldn't look more low-key than he did right now—and unthreatening.

He handed her more coffee.

"I found out far too late that one of the suspects forging art and selling it at auction on the black market…was my boyfriend. Chadwell."

Hank pressed his lips together. What kind of a ridiculous name was that?

He put their bowls in the sink and had her move to the living room with him. Instead of sitting, she petted Dax for a moment on his bed in the corner. Then she wandered to the credenza he'd inherited from his mom, while he sat in his recliner.

"When I realized he was the suspect, it all fit together that he'd lied to me. He was at one of the galleries where a theft occurred." She stared through the glass at his photos. Other small things he'd collected over the years. Ceramic mugs that reminded him of his mother. "And a hundred things I overlooked that I shouldn't have. So I confronted him."

Hank winced. "He hurt you?"

She turned, nodding. "Pushed me up against the wall. Shoved his arm against my throat. I tried to fight him off." She swallowed. "Used everything I had, and all the tricks my dad taught me on fighting dirty. I managed to hit him over the head with a lamp and nearly knock him out, just enough for me to run to the neighboring apartment. He was just getting home—an older man. He let me into his place and called the police."

Hank leaned forward on his recliner, forearms on his knees. "I'm so sorry that happened to you."

Alena nodded. "I never saw it. He fooled me completely."

"That doesn't make you a bad agent."

"Tell that to everyone I work with."

Maybe he should. "It just means you trusted the wrong guy, that's all. If the people you work with can't see that you're just a human like everyone is, then that's their flaw. It's not on you."

Alena turned back to the credenza. "Is that your team?" She pointed to a photo of him and his buddies. His squad and the K-9 he'd taken out on ops with them.

"Yep."

"And that guy?" She pointed to the framed photo of him and Evan.

"My brother."

"He was a marine also?"

"We got out around the same time." He tried to find a way to explain that whole thing. Sure, between them, they'd saved two lives. But the cost had been high and sometimes he wasn't sure he could live with it. "He lives on the other side of town and works for an armored truck company. I talked to him early this morning and he agreed to watch Kitty. I had Officer Stephans take Elizabeth's dog to his house."

Alena snorted. "And this?"

Hank groaned. He'd been hoping the discussion of the tiny dog that'd been tossed at her would distract her.

He pushed off the chair and walked over to stand beside her. Dax lifted his head, but Hank used a hand signal to tell him not to worry. To lie back down. "My wedding photo."

He stared at it. Sighed. Why hadn't he removed that as soon as they arrived last night?

"You're married?"

"Was. Been divorced four years."

"And you keep your wedding photo displayed."

Hank scratched his jaw. Yeah, he definitely should've put that out of sight. "A reminder. Not to trust the wrong person."

Alena twisted to face him.

"She lied. She cheated. She left me while I was deployed, but I didn't find out until I was back that she'd cleaned out our joint bank account." Thankfully she hadn't had full access to his trust. "She was in Mexico with her boyfriend."

"Wow."

Hank nodded.

"She had no clue what she had, did she?" Alena shook her head, a look of incredulity on her face. "Boy, I'd like to give her a piece of my mind."

Hank started to chuckle.

"I'm sure she realizes what she traded in, and she knows it was a huge mistake."

"Okay." Hank shook his head.

She was laying it on thick, making him laugh. They both needed something lighter, or the stress would drag them back to that place where their lives had fallen apart.

"I mean really. A man who makes potatoes like you—"

Hank tugged Alena to him and wrapped his arms around her in a hug. "Thank you."

She chuckled against his chest. "Two peas in a pod, we are."

"Sounds like a great—and miserable—friendship."

He felt her chuckle again. He didn't find it quite so amusing, given he thought it was entirely possible he wanted more than just friendship. Alena knew what it was like to trust the wrong person.

Was there a right person out there somewhere?

Or was she right in front of him?

Hank needed to figure out if he was willing to take the risk.

He pulled away just as his phone rang, back on the kitchen counter. "It might be Chief Willa."

She nodded, brushing back hair from her eyes. He took a deep breath and tamped down the rising feelings. Probably, it wasn't worth the risk. Things were good between them as colleagues and friends. Why potentially jeopardize that by making it more than it needed to be?

They'd both been hurt.

Taking a risk meant the chance it would happen over again. And since Hank couldn't stand the idea of going through that once more, let alone Alena being hurt when she'd nearly been attacked in one of the worst ways, there was no reason to push it.

His boss's name flashed on the screen. Hank answered, "Officer Miller."

"Good. Ready for an update?"

"Yes, sir. I'll put you on speaker and get Special Agent Sanchez in here." He waved her in and held the phone between them. "Go ahead, Chief."

"Carol is out of surgery but in ICU, she's fighting for her life. So say a prayer for her."

Hank said, "Yes, sir."

"I should have images from the hotel later this morning, a collection of photos of men who fit the description of both of the suspects. I'd like the two of you to come by and take a look. See if you can pick out the assailants you saw."

Alena said, "We can absolutely do that. And we'll listen to the recording from right before Carol was stabbed. See if we can hear anything on the feed that might tell us who tried to kill her."

Hank nodded, glad she wanted to refocus on the case. Things had segued into something more complicated, and personal. There were two dangerous men out there to find.

"Copy that. See you soon." Willa hung up.

Alena stood. "Time to get back to work."

TWELVE

Alena clicked through the computer menu and opened the program. They'd had her sit at a desk in the main bullpen of the Sundown Valley PD. Hank sat across the room at his desk. Conveniently where she could see him in her peripheral vision, just enough so that it distracted her from what she was doing.

She couldn't believe his ex-wife had cheated on him. That was so wrong. She shook her head for probably the eleventh time, baffled that any woman would do that to a guy like him. What had she been thinking?

Alena could hardly believe she'd told him about Chadwell. Then again, that was almost safer than the other secret she kept from him. Good thing it had nothing to do with this case.

Maybe they could find those two guys and she could leave with her privacy intact.

This marine she'd met didn't need to know what she'd managed to keep from everyone. It wasn't because she was embarrassed, it was simply for the best that she maintained her dad's reputation. Especially with a guy who'd served under him. Who could remember her dad the way he'd been, rather than see the man he was now.

Alena had put on her FBI uniform before they'd left Hank's house. Even though they didn't have a uniform, technically, she just wanted to feel professional. No point being any other way with everything that'd happened. She had to forget being held at gunpoint, forget the break-in of her room and everything else since she arrived at the resort. All of it needed to be pushed aside so they could figure out who had attempted to murder Carol.

The woman deserved nothing less than their best efforts at fighting for justice, whether she survived or if she sadly couldn't win that battle.

Elizabeth was in holding, ready to be interviewed.

The two men had to be ID'd and found.

Stolen jewels had to be returned.

They weren't at a loss for things to do. She didn't need to sit around and think about how Hank looked in his uniform, his dog asleep in the crate beside his desk.

Her phone vibrated.

Alena saw the caller's name and tugged her

earbuds from her backpack. She slid one in and toggled the button on screen to answer the call. "Good morning, Sandy."

The other woman's face filled the screen. Her shirt was a scrubs top, this one pink, which was the color she favored most of the time even if she switched it up regularly.

Sandy, the nurse Alena had hired, lived in the guest room at her father's house, the only reason Alena didn't worry constantly while she worked.

Across the room, Hank glanced over for a second. Alena held up one finger. He was supposed to come over and listen to the recording of the moments before Carol had been attacked, but they'd have to wait on that for a second.

"Alena, it's good to see you."

She hadn't told Sandy anything about what'd happened in Sundown Valley and she wouldn't. The woman wasn't privy to FBI cases. "How is he this morning?"

Sandy's expression softened. "Good. We went for a long walk yesterday, and I think we'll spend some time listening to that book we're reading right now."

Alena had to clear her throat. "That's good."

"I got a call from the local veteran's association. A couple of local guys who knew your father in the service would like to come by."

"Thanks." Alena had to figure out how to respond to requests like that. "Give me their number. I'll call back."

Sandy's expression shifted. "You can't keep people away forever."

Alena had to keep her voice low or everyone would hear. "They don't need to see him like this."

"I might argue otherwise."

"So you want to show him off? Subject him to their pity."

"Alena—"

She gritted her teeth, aware she was drawing attention to herself. "I can't talk about this right now. I'm working."

Sandy sighed. "Okay. How long do you think you'll be there?"

"A few days at most. Give or take this storm that has shut down the highway, I might not be able to find a flight." She didn't plan on looking for a flight out until this thing was over, since she had no idea how long the case would take. "I'll let you know as soon as I know."

Sandy nodded. "Okay, thanks. Do you want to say hi? I know he'd love to see your face."

"Sure." Alena got up and headed for the hall, where she found a quiet alcove. Her father came on the screen, a wonky smile on his face. "Hi, Dad. How are you?"

"Girl." His smile widened. "My girl."

After he'd had the stroke, her father had gotten frustrated trying to talk. They'd started with simple words, easy for him to pronounce. Even though he could say more now, thanks to working with a therapist, he'd stuck with calling her "girl."

"It's good to see you." Alena smiled. "I'll be home soon, okay?"

Sandy shifted the phone. "Take care of yourself."

Alena nodded. She tapped the screen and hung up. For a long moment, Alena leaned against the wall, her head back. She stared up at the ceiling and took stock of the aches and pains of the day. She closed her eyes and inhaled a long breath.

Why did You give me this to carry?

She felt like the world weighed down her shoulders. There was nothing she could do about it when shrugging off the thing she had to carry meant being the kind of person who gave up and walked away. Not who she wanted to be—and all too much like Hank's ex. Giving up out of selfishness. Going somewhere else, looking for something better, which would only turn out nothing like what she had.

Alena got to live with her father. She got to

take care of him, not just because of all the times he'd taken care of her.

"Hey." His voice was as soft as the touch of his hand on her shoulder. "You okay?"

Alena opened her eyes and nodded. "Sure. We should get back to it."

He said nothing, and didn't move, just kept studying her with that gentle expression. "You can talk about whatever is going on with you."

"It won't eliminate the danger here or help catch these two guys. It won't help Carol recover from the stabbing and go on to live the rest of her life."

"But it's important to you." Hank shifted slightly. "And I agree about working the case, but like earlier this morning, it is okay to talk about something else."

He actually wanted her to share? She didn't know if she even could.

Alena shook her head. "What's the point?"

Talking about her dad with the exact person she shouldn't? Not going to help. As much as she might want to open up and find support from a friend, this was her path to walk and no one else's. She had Sandy to connect with and help her take care of her father since the stroke. That was it.

She didn't need anyone else to know.

His expression shuttered. "Right. No point."

He stepped back. "Let's talk to Elizabeth. We need to know where Matthew and his friend might've gone. Then you can go back to your FBI life."

He thought this was about the divide between local PD and a federal agent? She'd hardly played that card, or kept that distance between them, through this. Or was it a natural function of their jobs that kept them separated. They were only working this case together because she'd come to his town.

Making her the interloper and him the one who could help—or not—and then watch her walk away.

He turned back at the end of the hall. "Are you coming, Special Agent Sanchez?"

Alena pushed off the wall. "This is my case, so I'm taking the lead on the interview."

Hank didn't bother responding to that. He wasn't going to argue with it either. Whoever took the lead on the interview, he didn't really care. She might be intent on carving out that divide between local and federal law enforcement, but he had no idea why.

He'd come over to tell her the officer had brought Elizabeth to an interview room. The fact he'd seen her after a clearly difficult phone call was the only reason he'd failed to mention it first.

Apparently, she didn't want him any further into her life than he already was. And if he was honest, that was for the best. Only, he couldn't help wondering. His career was stable, and enjoyable. His brother had actually answered the phone after Hank had sent a text that a dog needed watching. That almost made him smile right now, the look that would've been on Evan's face when the officer showed up with a Chihuahua. Romance hadn't been on his radar after his ex-wife. It seemed like Alena was the only woman who could've possibly changed his mind.

But she wasn't interested.

Hank lifted his chin at the officer on the door. "Thanks, Mike."

"Sure thing." The guy left his post and headed down the hall.

Hank opened the door to the interview room and stepped in, holding it wide so Alena could enter after him. He let her pick her seat on this side of the table, across from Elizabeth.

Alena sat. Hank opted to stand back, so he leaned against the wall and tried not to be mad, or disappointed, that Alena had basically blown him off. Not that now was the right time. But she was the first woman since his ex he'd even thought about in terms of what a relationship between them might be. Sure, they lived in different states, and it wouldn't work, but he couldn't even wonder?

As soon as the case was over, Alena would be going home.

"Elizabeth, I'm not going to lie to you or sugarcoat it," Alena began. "You're looking at serious jail time."

The other woman stared at Alena across the table, a look of defiance on her face. "I'm the victim here."

"You're an accessory to everything Matthew and Steve have done."

Hank said, "That means everything they're going to be charged with, you'll also be charged with. There's no way to skate out from under the consequences."

Regardless of whether her lawyer argued she'd been under duress, Elizabeth would face some kind of penalty for the crimes she'd committed.

Alena said, "The power you have lies in what you can tell us. You've waived your right to counsel—"

"I don't need a lawyer telling me what I already know."

"Then it's up to you to listen and understand what I'm saying to you." Alena paused. "Every bit of useful information you can give us about what's already happened, and what Matthew and Steve are going to do next, will count in your favor. Information you give us that leads to their capture means we can argue with the prosecutor that you should face lesser charges."

"Maybe you should come back and ask what I know when you can make me a deal for no jail time."

Hank gritted his teeth. It would take time they didn't have to meet with the prosecutor—especially if they needed a federal one—and get the paperwork for that drawn up.

"If you're asking for zero jail time, you'd better hope you have something good." Alena leaned back in her chair. "So far, you haven't given us anything at all, let alone credible intel that is actually helpful to us. We need to find Matthew and Steve before they hurt anyone else. Before they leave town."

Elizabeth stared at her.

Hank wasn't going to allow her to skate out of this without talking. "You might not have seen what they did to Carol, but we did."

Alena leaned forward slightly. "Was it Matthew who stabbed her, or Steve?"

Elizabeth shrugged.

"Steve, before he targeted that other woman and stole her million-dollar necklace? Or Matthew, before he dragged me down to the basement level where he was going to shoot me?"

"I don't know." Elizabeth gritted her teeth.

"So what do you know?" Alena said. "Because, otherwise, there's not much I can do for you. You'll spend years in prison, and you'll probably never see your dog again."

Elizabeth gasped. Something else ghosted across her expression. Hank couldn't figure out what it was before it was gone.

He pushed off the wall and went to stand by the table. "You said they already had the jewels. Where would they go after the job is done?"

Elizabeth looked aside. "I only overheard them talking about transportation. And a rendezvous, whatever that is."

"Do you know where they're supposed to meet up?" Hank figured they weren't going far, since the storm and the heavy fall of snow last night had caused the freeway and highways in and out of town to be shut down. The same reason Alena's backup couldn't make it by car or plane into the small airport at the edge of town.

"They were going to send a group text."

Alena pushed her chair back and stood. "So you have nothing useful and we're wasting our time, I guess."

Hank took a step away from the table.

"I know *something*. I don't know nothing,

okay?" Elizabeth's tone rose to a higher pitch. "Someone on staff at the resort was the one helping them get everything packed up and out of there. And I'll tell you who it is."

Hank turned back. "Does that person know where to find them?"

Elizabeth frowned. "I don't know. Maybe?"

He let out a sigh. "How big is the haul? A duffel bag. A truckload?" There were options for either and the more information he could get from her, the better they could plan their next move.

"There were fifteen fake pieces in two suit-cases."

"Yours and Carol's?" Alena shifted closer to the table, almost brushing his shoulder with hers.

Elizabeth nodded.

"But your guy, Steve, went back for a neck-lace that didn't have a fake to switch it out with?" Alena asked.

"He said he couldn't resist the payday. We were gonna retire in Miami."

Hank wasn't entirely sure the plan had been to take her with him. Seemed more like Steve had split. Matthew had run out of the basement without killing Alena. Maybe because Steve had the necklace—or because he'd discovered his partner was about to leave without him.

Hank asked, "Will they leave together and split the proceeds, or kill each other to be the one left standing with the entire haul?"

Elizabeth flinched.

"Your personal choices of a boyfriend aside," Alena said, "do you think they'll kill each other?"

"Steve never mentioned Matthew when we talked about retirement."

Hank said, "Would he kill him, or just ditch him?"

Maybe they should just wait for the carnage and clean up after. Let the two men take care of each other, as neither of them was innocent. But the risk of someone else being caught in the crossfire was too great. He couldn't stand by on the off chance this would resolve itself if it ended up costing someone else a loved one.

Elizabeth swallowed. "Steve will kill him, take the necklace and the jewels."

"Who at the resort is in on it?"

She blanched at Hank's question. "He works in the office."

Alena said, "That's it?"

"I don't know his name."

Alena headed out of the room. Hank followed, and the officer came back to watch the room to make sure Elizabeth didn't go anywhere. She strode down the hall back toward the bullpen. "Both of them are dangerous."

Hank didn't have a chance to respond. Chief Willa walked out of his office. "Listen up, everyone."

Hank caught the air of tension in the room. Dax stood in his crate, his nose to the door.

"What is it, Chief?"

"We just got a call. An armored truck was robbed in town. Both guards have been kidnapped and they took everything inside."

"An armored truck." Alena turned to Hank, a frown on her face.

"That's how the resort contact transported the jewels off the property."

"And now they have all the jewelry."

Hank said, "And the guards as hostages."

THIRTEEN

Even though Hank was the one driving, it was better to be headed somewhere. Doing something. Working the case. That was far more preferable to having downtime. Running background and trying to squeeze more information out of Elizabeth so they could finally ID Steve and Matthew and put out an alert to all local law enforcement to be on the lookout for them.

Hank hadn't said much after he'd told her he was loading Dax into his crate in the back. Alena glanced around and saw the dog's attention on her. She reached back and put her fingers against the wire. His tongue flicked out and licked the tips of her fingers.

Alena smiled. "I've never had a dog."

Hank glanced over. According to the GPS, they were only a few minutes from where the armored truck had been abandoned. "Never?"

She shook her head. "My dad and I moved around too much, and neither of us wanted a puppy home alone all day. Years ago, at one point, we had neighbors whose puppy made a mess on all their beds when it had an upset stomach."

Hank winced. "That sounds nasty."

"I could smell their house from my back-yard."

"And now? You know Dax isn't a pet. He's a police dog."

Alena studied the animal. "He seems to just want to work."

Hank chuckled. "The trick is convincing him we should take a day off. But he is a Lab, so he can't take too many days off, or he gets used to that weekend life."

Alena smiled, but only to herself.

The frost between them that made the K-9 patrol car feel colder than it probably was hadn't lifted. Still, the banter was nice. Talking about something light, not about the heaviness that filled the air after she'd spoken to Sandy and her father.

No point rehashing all that. What was there to say? Hank probably had parts of his life he didn't need to share with her when she would leave town as soon as the case was over. Neither of them was going to give up their job. That's all there was to it.

The only reason they were still working this

case together was Chief Willa's order that Hank continue to look out for her.

He pulled onto a side street not far from the main drag of shops. Roads were reasonably clear, even with the new snow. "The central street in Sundown Valley is mostly hundred-year-old buildings on both sides of the street, a redbrick spot where the bank has always been, and newer businesses like the bakery. It's closed for the season. That's a local community church. They meet in a storefront."

He turned behind the bank building and she spotted a rear entrance. The armored truck had been parked at an angle, both doors still open. Two marked police cars with flashing lights flanked it but stayed back. A silver Volvo approached from the far end of the back alley.

Hank parked. He made a "huh" noise in the back of his throat and pushed out of the car.

Alena did the same and met him at the back door. "Everything okay?"

"The truck company sent over their supervisor." He barely paused a beat before he said, "Evan Miller. My brother."

Alena frowned. "I thought he was watching Elizabeth's dog."

"He is." Hank let Dax hop out, and the three of them headed for the huddle.

Alena held her hand out to the officers first,

introducing herself. She saved Evan until last. "You're the representative from the armored truck company, and Hank's brother?"

"Evan Miller, nice to meet you." He wore tan khakis and a polo, over which he'd pulled an SDV Security windbreaker. His nose and ears would be red if they were out here much longer.

The wind was cold enough Alena found herself stomping her feet and crossing her arms just to retain some warmth. She needed fleece-lined work pants for this town. Except for her overcoat, she'd dressed to work in the office.

He said, "Couple of days, it'll be back up to the forties and it'll feel like spring." Only a hint of nervousness in his expression. "Let's see what the van security can tell us."

Hank took a step closer into their huddle. "You could've emailed the police department the footage."

Evan shrugged. "I want to be here to help in person. It's better for business."

"It's also freezing."

Evan chuckled. There was something a little rougher about him than there was about Hank. The younger brother had an edgy side that helped her understand why Hank had found it so amusing he was watching Elizabeth's dog.

The last thing she needed was to be distracted by Hank's brother, of all people. There was a case to solve, more than one missing guard, and jewels to return to their rightful owners. Not to mention bringing in Matthew and Steve before they hurt anyone else.

Alena said a prayer in that moment. There were far too many unknowns, loose threads, and potential ways this could go wrong and end up deadly. They needed God's hand to be on this. Only when she was submitted to what He wanted could she trust the outcome completely. Whatever happened, and however things turned out, He was still good.

"Let's see what's on the van security footage." Alena turned to the vehicle then asked one of the uniformed officers, "What was taken?"

He strode over and they took a look at the back of the van. Rows of bins had been pulled out and dumped on the floor. A couple of lockboxes on the floor right behind the front seats were open, left that way. "Near as we can tell, it was pretty much cleaned out. A bracelet looks like it was dropped." He pointed. "There, in the middle of the floor, by that velvet pouch."

"I see it." She scanned the interior. "And the security company can tell us what was being transported?" She asked loudly enough that Evan should've heard her, but he looked to be in deep conversation with Hank. And neither looked happy. "Guys?"

Evan turned to her. "I have my laptop. It should be able to hook directly into the van's internal security system. We have a camera in the cab that should show us what happened." He rotated his computer so that it folded open instead of closed, leaving the keyboard resting on his hand and the screen on top.

Evan tapped the screen then used a cord from his pocket to plug the laptop into the computer mounted in the truck.

"Looks like they destroyed the company laptop." Alena wasn't optimistic it would show them what had happened.

"Shouldn't matter." Evan tapped the screen again with his finger. "They didn't destroy the hard drive just smashing it. Those things are tough." His phone beeped. "Hold this." Evan handed Hank his laptop, much to his brother's surprise, and walked away to take a call.

Hank sighed. "He could focus."

"Maybe the call is related to this." Alena wanted to know what the deal was between the two brothers, but given she hadn't shared with him what her issue was after talking to Sandy and her dad, she couldn't exactly ask. She'd drawn a line between them that meant personal issues were off-limits. "Can we look at the video feed?"

Hank glanced at the screen. "I'd have no idea

where to start. Evan always was better at this stuff."

His brother came back over then. "The head of human resources followed up on the two guards scheduled for this truck today. One never showed up for work last night. They got on shift at midnight, but he says he got a call they weren't needed."

Evan reached over and tapped the screen while Hank held it. "Two guys in the vehicle. Per policy." He frowned. "The head of HR is calling the shop supervisor to find out who the second man was."

Alena figured she could guess. "So they took the jewels from the resort. One of our thieves posed as a guard and babysat the transport."

Why get himself on the truck? Wouldn't the partner, or someone else, have known he shouldn't be there?

She continued, "It's a decent way to securely transport merchandise. No one would think twice about the truck. If we thought there were thieves at the resort we'd be looking at surveillance of anyone leaving carrying a bag—not an official transport. But why would your employee not say something?"

"That's what I'd like an answer to." Evan frowned. "I sincerely hope our missing guard didn't do something he shouldn't have."

A look passed between the two brothers. Tension and a whole lot of animosity.

Alena said, "Whatever that is, set it aside."

Hank felt Dax shift against his side. He shuffled the laptop in his hands. "We need to see what happened in the cab of this truck."

Evan said nothing. The look they shared had been enough that Alena caught on to it. Now he looked like a hypocrite after he got mad at her for her not sharing her personal deal with him. Looked like that should go both ways.

If it was going to happen.

A man was missing and the two they were chasing were likely involved.

Alena moved close and watched as the feed came on, starting from the present moment. Evan toggled it back to a spot where they could see two men in the seats, then let it play. "That's the guard who is supposed to be driving," Evan said. "He's newer, but we've never had any problems with him before."

One of the officers said, "Give us his information, we can contact his next of kin and whoever he's closest to. Make sure they're aware of what's happening." He looked at Hank. "And the detectives can do a full rundown on his financials. Social media. Things like that."

Hank nodded. They needed to see if he'd been

in a situation recently that made him vulnerable to blackmail, or if he'd done this expecting a payout that would resolve an outstanding debt. Maybe gambling. It was possible this guy had been targeted at random, was someone who just happened to be in the wrong place at the wrong time. But there was a reason the other guard for today's shift had been told to stay home.

This one was the weak link.

Evan said, "I know who my guy is. But who is the passenger? I've never seen him before in my life."

"That's Matthew." Alena's voice had an edge to it. Not exactly fear, more the lingering memory of all that rushing adrenaline. Having no weapon when faced with an armed man intent on killing her. She'd done well, drawing him away from innocents and hiding. Had he told her that?

"I chased Matthew from that hallway. But neither of us has seen the second man." Hank sighed. They needed an image to run for facial recognition. Not having one for either man was frustrating, to say the least. Kind of like this whole case—and trying to grow trust between him and Alena.

The second man was still out there, and the hotel no longer had security footage. Even though they were supposed to be sending over images of people at the check-in desk in case they could identify their suspect that way, Hank had no idea how they'd tell who he was.

"Okay, then." Alena blew out a breath. "Here's what we do know. Matthew talked or bribed his way onto this truck because this is how they got the jewels from the resort to…wherever they were going. Maybe here, or maybe this wasn't the plan. We don't know."

Were the two men double-crossing each other? There wasn't much else that made sense. Maybe at this point it was every man for himself, and both Matthew and Steve were vying for the jewels. Using creative ways to escape with them—like the armored truck.

"Whatever the plan was, they can't get out of town right now. That gives us more time to find them here." Hank caught Evan looking at him but didn't get the look on his face. "Hit Play."

Evan refocused on the screen, still in Hank's grasp. They watched the video. Matthew said something they couldn't hear, as the video had no audio. Then he swung out suddenly with a gun in his hand and slammed it into the driver's head.

Evan hissed. Maybe he'd been away from action awhile, so that seeing something like this was shocking to him.

"Is the vic a friend of yours?" Hank didn't

want his brother to be so scared for his friend that it affected their ability to find the guy. He also wanted to know if Evan was personally connected—more than just as the supervisor.

Evan seemed to be doing well for himself. Despite not calling Hank back earlier.

"Doesn't matter." Evan said, "Is this a case you're working?"

Alena was the one who said, "Yes, mine. Your brother is protecting me until it's done."

He looked back at the screen in time to see Matthew shove his door open, grab the other man's jacket and haul him out of the van.

"He took a hostage." Hank's stomach flipped over. On the video, he spotted something when the guard's legs dropped out of the door. "Hold this." He dumped the laptop in Evan's hands and clicked his fingers for Dax. He'd clipped on the leash for the simple fact this was a crime scene and Dax wasn't friendly with everyone he met, but for the most part they didn't need it.

What they needed right now was a run. Just the two of them. And lunch after.

Hank's stomach rumbled. In the passenger footwell of the truck, he found what he was looking for. "Gloves!"

One of the officers jogged over and handed him some. Hank used them to pick up the shoe left on the floor mat, praying Dax could get a scent. That Matthew hadn't had a vehicle waiting nearby—the one thing Dax couldn't follow—and that the guard was still alive.

He grasped his radio and called in the start of a search, giving their location and the situation. Dax sat his doggy behind on the ground so fast, Hank nearly laughed. He knew what the word "search" meant even in the midst of a bunch of other words.

His K-9's tail wagged, all his attention focused on Hank, who checked everything and mentally ran through the surrounding area and where Matthew might have taken the other man. Had they gone far?

Hank signed off and crouched. "Dax. Get it."

His dog pretty much stuffed his nose in the shoe. He sniffed all around it, thoroughly absorbing the scent of the guard he would track until they found the guy.

Then he sat.

"Ready?" Hank shifted the leash in his fingers and braced to run. "Dax. Seek."

FOURTEEN

Alena watched Dax sniff around on the ground, turning in a circle some until he zeroed in on what he was looking for.

"He found it." Evan used a low voice, maybe so it didn't disturb the K-9.

Hank and Dax set off at a decent pace, a little faster than a stroll but not quite a jog. Alena followed, hanging back but sticking with them. Not because Hank was supposed to be protecting her. Not even really because this was a fresh lead on her case.

She was drawn to him.

Hank had so much strength and focus in him. He knew who he was and what he should be doing. Dax was adorable—and professional.

"They're good, right?"

Alena glanced to the side, where Evan kept in step with her. "Hank and Dax?"

Evan nodded. "He's worked with dogs for years. Sniffing out IEDs, making an area safe

for the people who live there. Kids playing soc-
cer in a village. Or the unit going on patrol."
There was a wistfulness to his voice. Hank's
brother was a little in awe of who he was. They
were the only family each other had left, since
Hank had told her his parents had been killed
in a small plane crash, and the grandmother
they'd been sent to live with had passed away.

Kind of like her and her father, it was just the
two of them.

She could understand that family dynamic.

It wasn't her business to suss out what it was
that made it seem like something was off between them. A tiny discordant note in their relationship.

"Dax is special." Evan paused then said,
"Though, maybe every dog is in its own way.
Except that Chihuahua in my bathroom. Prob-
ably chewing up the rug."

Up ahead, the K-9 sniffed along the street.
Hank followed after him, completely focused
on his partner and the cues Dax would give him.

"What's ahead of us?" She figured Evan
could tell her and she wouldn't have to disturb
Hank's concentration.

Matthew couldn't have taken a freaked-out
man wearing one shoe, maybe dazed from the
hit, too far. Especially not because he was hauling
all the jewels with him. Maybe in a duffel bag?

She prayed that Matthew didn't cut his losses and simply kill the guard he had hostage. There had already been enough pain so far.

Evan glanced around. "We're behind the grocery store. The high school is up ahead, a couple of streets down. Mostly this area is residential though. The people in town who live here year-round walk to work and school a lot—especially when the weather is bad. They clear the roads, but that just piles the snow at the end of people's driveways, and it takes too long to dig a car out."

Alena said a prayer for any innocent person in Matthew's path. Not just the guard he'd kidnapped, or strung along like they were partners, but anyone on the street or in their home who might get caught in the crossfire.

Matthew was capable of anything. She'd seen him attempting to strangle Carol, he was her most likely suspect for the stabbing, and he'd tried to kill her as well. He must be holding on to the guard to use as a bargaining chip.

Dax picked up his pace then stopped beside a chain-link fence.

"He's found something," Hank called back. "Looks like a necklace."

Alena didn't have any evidence bags and there wasn't much she could do about that.

Hank radioed in to one of the officers back

at the armored truck, and requested someone to head over, document and collect the piece. She took several photos of the item with her phone, just for her own records, before Hank and Dax continued on.

"Seek, Dax. Seek."

The dog resumed sniffing, leading them in a path along the sidewalk.

"They went a ways on foot," Evan said.

"That probably means Matthew didn't have a plan. Or he'd have parked a car close by." Alena thought for a moment.

Hank had chased Matthew after he hurt Carol in the hallway. He'd seen the car.

"We have one car everyone is watching for. Maybe that burned it," Alena said. "He can't use it now, so he had to dump it and hasn't stolen another one yet."

"Could be the guard has one and that's where they're headed." Evan pulled out his phone. "I'll call the head of HR. Find out if he lives nearby."

Alena watched Hank and Dax while Evan made the call. It seemed odd this was where she'd wound up, rather than spending the weekend undercover. Gathering information to pass back to her team so they could finally ID the people on this crew of thieves.

Instead she'd wound up with a K-9 team that specialized in Search and Rescue and her case had exploded into so much more than she'd been expecting. Rather than be comfortable with what she was here to do this weekend, she'd been thrown into something risky and intense.

Almost as if God had wanted to test her trust in Him. After all, that was how her faith in Him grew—not through being comfortable but through being stretched. She had no choice but to face what happened this weekend and rely on His strength to do it.

Like she'd had no other choice but to take care of her father. Keep his newsletter going herself, even when she didn't exactly know what she was doing. Face the worst of her failures as an FBI agent. Take a step forward in spite of the fear of the unknown, or her own inadequacies.

Evan hung up. "He lives on the other side of town, so I don't think they're headed for his house."

That didn't rule out a storage unit or some other place where Matthew could steal a car from him. "What's his name?"

"Wallace Campbell. He's twenty, and he just proposed to his girlfriend at Thanksgiving."

Alena winced. Not that it was worse when a person had loved ones versus someone who was a loner. Someone with a family wasn't inherently more valuable than someone who lived alone. Still, there was a woman whose life might be irrevocably changed today. "We need to find him."

"Looks like they're headed for the high school." Evan pointed up the street, where another chain-link fence started. She could see a gap, presumably a path students used to get on and off campus.

Dax picked up his pace. He slowed suddenly, turning one way then the other.

Hank said, "Something happened here. But I don't see anything else was dropped."

The K-9 set off again.

He led them all the way to the fence then onto the high school campus.

Alena scanned the area, not seeing anyone over by the buildings. Between them and the concrete structures was a huge field covered in a thin layer of snow packed down with boots over several days. Dax headed along the fence line toward a storage shed.

She frowned. Was someone in the shed? If Wallace somehow got away, would he have hidden inside? The alternative was that Matthew had killed him and dumped his body in this shed.

Dax headed right for the door.

Alena said a prayer. When Evan added, "Amen," she realized she'd said it out loud.

Dax sat by the shed door. Hank rubbed his

muzzle. "Good boy, Dax. Good boy." He drew his gun. Alena did the same, covering him while he opened the door. Alena looked inside, gun first in case it was Matthew in there waiting for them.

A young man sat slumped against the back wall, his shoulder up against a riding lawn mower. Blood ran from a gash on his temple. She holstered her weapon and crouched beside him. Alena pressed two fingers to his carotid and felt a heartbeat. "He's alive."

Alena patted his shoulder. "Wallace, can you hear me?"

Hank backed away from the shed door and radioed the dispatcher that the guard had been found. His brother glanced between Hank and Alena, assessing them. Almost like he didn't know what to make of them. Hank asked for an ambulance as soon as it could get there.

Once he'd finished, Evan said, "You two make a pretty good team." He motioned between Hank and Alena, probably so Hank didn't think his brother was talking about Dax. Then he walked over to the dog. "Can I pet him?"

Hank nodded.

"You're a good boy, Dax." Evan gave him a rubdown, head to tail. "Yes, you are, Officer Dax."

Hank moved to the door of the shed so he could see Alena. "Is Wallace awake?"

"He's trying."

"Ambulance will be here in a minute." He walked far enough away that he could see the back side of the shed, just to make sure Matthew hadn't gone there.

"You think he's here?" Evan had never been so interested in what Hank did. In fact, since they'd both left the military around the same time, Hank had always assumed his brother probably wanted to be a cop. He hadn't been able to get the job due to his other-than-honorable discharge. Something Hank should've walked away with instead.

"I doubt it, but I have to be sure. It affects all of our safety if there's a dangerous, armed man still hanging around."

Evan nodded. "Right."

An ambulance siren preceded the vehicle, flashing lights reflecting off the snow and the school building. Hank clicked on his flashlight and waved them through the break in the fence. Two EMTs he'd seen already in the past couple days. "Hey, guys."

The older EMT carried a packed red duffel. "You're stacking them up this weekend."

Hank figured that was true enough, even if

it wasn't his doing. "At least so far it hasn't resulted in a death."

The second EMT had the yellow backboard. "Let's keep it that way."

"In there."

Both men disappeared into the shed. Alena stepped out. "He woke up a little."

Hank assessed her, taking from her his cue on whether to be worried this guy would die or if the guard was going to be all right. "Did he say anything?"

Alena kept her expression tight. "Not much. Matthew shoved him around, surprised him."

Evan stepped into their huddle and set his hand on Dax's head. "Did he say whether the guy paid him or if he wasn't involved?"

Hank was about to ask if this was the time to worry about company liability when Alena said, "I don't know it's enough to conclude either way at this stage. But he should be alive tomorrow to answer whatever questions you have."

Evan reached up and grasped the back of his neck. He blew out a breath. "I didn't think this was going to happen on my Sunday."

Hank said, "None of us did. But we need to catch this guy before he hurts someone else—or gets away with this."

The EMTs came out of the shed, walking the injured guard between them. His eyes were glassy, but he focused on Hank and the rest of them while they helped him.

"Can we ask him a couple of questions?" Hank figured it didn't hurt to make the request. Otherwise, they had no idea where Matthew had gone—or what he planned to do next.

The EMT said, "Let's get him in the ambulance."

"Thanks." Alena followed them.

"She's quite a woman." Evan scratched at his jaw.

"Don't even think about it."

"Because you're calling dibs?"

Hank nearly throttled his little brother right then and there, even though he hadn't had the urge to do that in years. "Bro, that's the most juvenile thing you could've said right now."

"That doesn't mean no." Evan said, "And I'm not wrong about her, am I?"

"Can we do this later?"

Evan sighed. "Look, I know I've been AWOL lately."

Hank winced. Evan realized what he'd said and did the same. Hank said, "We should hang out and talk. Probably soon."

"I do want to. Things at work have been crazy, and you're in the middle of something right now. It can wait." Evan held out his hand. "I just wanna catch up."

Hank grabbed his brother's hand and pulled him in for a hug. "Me, too. So why don't you call me?"

"Okay." Evan pointed at the ambulance. "Send me a text and update me on this, yeah?" Hank nodded.

Evan said, "I'll leave you to it."

He turned and walked away, almost like he took some of the knot that resided in Hank's stomach with him when he left. It wasn't better that they stayed apart though. Estrangement hadn't ever worked for them. They were the only family each other had left, until either of them got married. They needed to figure out their stuff.

Hank strode to the back of the ambulance where Alena stood watching them get Wallace settled. The guard was fully awake now, responding to questions.

The older EMT climbed out. "Make it fast."

"We just need to know if the guy who took him said anything, or if he knows where he went." Hank stood with the EMT while Alena climbed in and spoke to the victim.

Evan hadn't been wrong in his assessment of her. Hank was seriously attracted, and if their lives meshed at all, he'd have been all in for figuring out how to make a relationship work. Not just because she was the first woman he'd met since his ex-wife had broken his heart and destroyed his trust that made him want to try.

Had God brought her here for a reason?

He tried to let the Lord direct his life and stay flexible in case He was trying to do something. What was the point in being rigid and immovable if it meant he missed what God might have for him? His heart wanted to move Alena from the "dream" column to the "reality" column.

"He told me the guy had jewelry from the armored truck," the EMT said. "That he stole it all from his partner."

Hank nodded. "Plenty of people will come out of the woodwork if they find out there's a payday to be had."

"All they've gotta do is kill the guy holding it."

"That's why I like this town." Hank turned to the EMT. "There aren't many people living here who would do that."

Except it was looking more and more like Matthew and Steve might be fighting each other. No one wanted the carnage that might bring if things got out of hand and innocents were caught in the crossfire.

"That's what happens when there's weird weather." The guy grinned. "Makes people do all kinds of things they wouldn't normally." He slapped Hank's shoulder and headed for the driver's door.

Alena climbed out of the ambulance a minute later. "He said Matthew was ranting. About how he was going to kill his partner and 'get the necklace.'"

"Any idea where he thinks he's going to find Steve?"

Alena nodded. "The airport."

Whether or not Matthew thought he could fly out when every plane in town had been grounded and nothing was flying in for at least twenty-four hours, they still had to go check it out. Maybe there was a spot at the airport, or nearby, where they'd planned to wait out the weather.

Hank tightened his grip on Dax's leash. "We need to get there before there's any more bloodshed, or innocent victims dragged into this."

FIFTEEN

Hank used a side gate to get them into the tiny local airport, explaining who they were. "I'll call if I need backup."

The guy nodded. "I've got a guy out doing the rounds. He'll help if you need it."

"Thanks." He pulled the car through the gate.

Alena hung up her call. "Okay, that's done."

"I've got an extra vest in my trunk." He took the small lane to the right, where the hangars had been built in a row that looked onto the runway.

"Thanks." Alena might be in a holding pattern until she left, but she could appreciate what she did have with Hank. A partnership of sorts and someone to watch her back. The way she'd take his if it came to that. "Not just for the vest, and for swinging by your house so I could change, but for everything this weekend. You've looked out for me, helped me work the case, and gave me somewhere to stay last night."

He pulled into a parking space in the lot beside the first hangar. "You're welcome. It definitely hasn't been boring, and now I've added the fact you can change your clothes in less than two minutes to the list of interesting things about you."

She watched his lips widen into a smile, thinking about kissing him. That definitely wasn't appropriate right now—or helpful. She couldn't help how her heart felt about this good man. Still, she could be a professional. "No, it hasn't been boring."

Dax sniffed through the grate of his kennel.

Alena turned to the dog. "Same to you, Dax." She felt the pull of a smile. "We should go take a look around."

"Yep." Hank pushed his door open.

Alena tugged on the vest, left her suit jacket in his car and slipped her coat back on.

"Hat or gloves?"

"It is getting cold." She'd put a thermal layer on under her jeans, and a long-sleeved T-shirt with a hoodie and her coat. Still, she said, "I'll take a beanie, if you have one."

Once they were ready and Dax was leashed up, they walked beside each other to the first hangar. Beyond it, there was a structure with the doors rolled open and light spilling out. She figured that was likely their destination and she half expected to hear gunshots from inside. Or the motor of an airplane engine.

The runway looked like a sheet of ice. It glinted in the light, beautiful but deadly.

There was no way Matthew could expect to leave town this way. Or on any of the closed roads. His best tactic would be to hike out if he really needed to go. Snowshoes would work, but that method was arduous and he would sweat his way to hypothermia.

Alena said, "If he has half a brain, he'll go back to the resort and stay a couple of nights holed up where no one will see him."

"If he does, we have a shot at catching him." Hank glanced over. "Do you think Wallace was lying?"

"No, he seemed sincere—and traumatized." Alena thought back to their conversation in the ambulance. "He just seemed like a scared young guy caught up in something terrible."

She wouldn't be completely surprised if he'd been paid off to call his partner and tell him not to show up for work—or have someone else do it. If he'd been leaned on to get Matthew on the truck. He could turn out to be a weak link these thieves had exploited. However, it seemed more like he might've been dragged into it with no clue what was happening. As far as she was concerned, that was just as likely.

Alena approached the hangar with the light spilling out. Before she managed to look inside, a crash resounded through the huge building. She flattened her back against the wall.

"I'll take the front," Hank whispered. "You find a back entrance in case he runs."

Alena figured Matthew was highly likely to do that when he realized they were here. "Copy. I'll wait until I hear you go in."

Hank nodded. She stared at him for a long second, but there was nothing to say or do that would change anything between them.

She walked away, jogging between hangars, looking for another way in. If things were at all different between them, she might have lifted up onto the balls of her feet and pressed a kiss to his cheek—or his lips. But she didn't have the right to do that. And when she was soon leaving, it would be unfair. They weren't having a vacation fling before school started up again, and neither were they teenagers with no cares in the world.

She needed to do her job and get back to her life. Back to where her father's church was, so she could go with him like she'd avoided doing for so long. She didn't need to waste moments wondering what it might be like to move her life—and her father—here. Find out what-if.

Alena located a back door. Unlocked.

If being there through her father's stroke had taught her anything, it was that reality had to be dealt with. And she loved being able to make sure he was cared for—and to care for him herself when she could. There was no point wishing for things to be different.

Gun first. Then she looked in. The hall was empty. Alena eased the door closed behind her and proceeded toward the main interior of the warehouse—which she presumed to be the door at the end of this hall. There could be two men here, so she had to watch her back.

She passed a closed door, no window. Some kind of office. The need to be out there watching Hank's back pressed her forward.

Alena twisted the handle on the door at the end and held her gun out with her other hand. An office, windows on the far side, where she could see a plane in the hangar and someone who might've been Matthew beside it, but it was too far to tell.

At the edge of her awareness, she heard a low moan. Coming from inside the office? She wasn't sure, but she could check it out. She just had to get through this room without being seen and she could ascertain what was making that noise.

Alena started to ease the door open. Someone slammed into it and her from behind, crushing her gun hand between the door and the frame. The gun tumbled from her hand. She bit back a reflexive cry and swung out with her off hand.

He grabbed her other wrist, pinning her.

Alena tried to turn around, but he still had her hand in the door. She cried out.

He backed off the door, still grasping her other wrist. She got her hand out and turned to see who it was.

Everything in her froze. Dark, malicious eyes stared back at her from a face she'd loved. Once. He was here. That meant… She should… Her thoughts flitted from one issue to the next so fast she didn't finish one before her mind moved to the next, refusing to settle.

"Chadwell." Her voice dripped with anger.

His eyes glinted with satisfaction.

Everything in her hated him, even though she was supposed to have moved on. Truth was, she would've said she'd moved on. "What are you…?"

Chadwell grabbed a handful of her hair. She tried to move but he was too fast.

Her ex slammed her head against the wall.

Hank.

Everything went black.

Hank unclipped Dax's leash and left it on the ground outside. He clicked his fingers, and when Dax looked at him, he used the hand motion for Stay. He eased forward and looked into the hangar.

A white two-person plane was parked inside. Older-looking, it probably belonged to a local or a hobbyist. Not the kind of person who would volunteer to fly someone in this weather. Maybe planes were taking off and landing at the regional airport, but it was likely equipped with deicer trucks. No one here needed to get anywhere urgently enough to offer to pay for something like that.

They could just fly out commercial, anyway.

Someone had opened the door to the plane and the stairs were lined up for access. He couldn't see anyone inside. Dax shifted in his sit and Hank was pretty sure the dog peered around his leg to look as well. He was about to signal his K-9 partner and go in when someone exited the plane.

Matthew jogged down the stairs in jeans and a jacket, his nose and ears red from the cold. He thought he was going to leave?

Dax let out a low growl that was carried away on the winter wind.

Matthew headed for a door at the far end. Windows beside the door would have showcased the office, but the light from the hangar reflected against the opaque glass so he couldn't see inside. Matthew would see him coming if Hank tried to sneak up behind him. He needed to wait for the guy to enter the office before he crept in.

Once he'd slapped cuffs on Matthew, he could find out where the jewels were, but the priority was both of the men involved.

He only saw Matthew right now. Not the man who'd gone by "Steve."

Matthew disappeared into the office. Hank patted the side of his leg, a signal that meant Heel that he used because sometimes he wore gloves, which made clicking his fingers impossible. He moved left and took the long way in case Matthew looked out the office windows.

Hank jogged through the hangar. He expected to hear Alena call out, as she should've been in the back by now. Had she not found an open door? Maybe they shouldn't have split up, but for right now he was going to trust her. Covering both exits was standard procedure, and she was an FBI agent.

Inside the office, he heard a muffled yell.

As he approached the door from the opposite side, something slammed against the glass from the inside—which turned out to be durable like a car windshield. The clear plate of the window bowed and he heard Matthew yell, "Yes, you are. Or you die. So choose."

Hank twisted the door handle slowly, listening to muffled conversation

Dax entered first.

Hank yelled, "Catch!"

The K-9 clamped on to Matthew's arm with his powerful bite and the weight of his body dragged the man's arm off the guy he had up against the window.

Matthew cried out. He tried to kick against Dax, but the dog dragged him to the ground. Hank closed in, his weapon pointed at the bad guy who'd nearly killed Alena. "Don't. You won't like what happens."

"Get him off me!"

"Don't move." Hank let Matthew settle. "Dax, release."

The dog let go of his bite on the man's arm but didn't back up. He stayed where he was and growled at the man on the floor.

The one who'd been up against the window slumped down, hands bound. A gag over his mouth that explained the muffled voice.

Matthew clutched his arm, which wasn't bleeding. "Your dog is gonna kill me!"

"That's not in his job description." Hank had him roll to his face and put his hands behind his back. "I'll get you medical attention forthwith. If you cooperate."

Matthew did as instructed. Hank secured his

hands behind his back and assisted him to stand. He stuck the guy in a chair to sit—after he relieved him of the weapons he was carrying. "Sir, you okay?" Hank asked the other man.

The guy nodded. Hank set Dax to guard Matthew, then went and took the man's gag off his mouth. "You're the pilot?"

"I'm not taking off on an icy runway. It's suicide."

"Agreed." Hank got his hands untied. "Do you have a phone to call 9-1-1 here?"

He didn't want to hand over his own cell if there was a working phone here. He needed to keep hold of it for himself.

He helped the man to his feet and the pilot used the desk phone. Hank turned to Matthew. "Where is your partner, Steve?"

Matthew made a face. Belligerence bled through his expression.

"Guess it doesn't matter now. He's going to get away with that necklace and all the rest of the jewels, whether you like it or not. He'll be free to do whatever he wants while you rot in prison for the rest of your life."

Hank pulled out his phone and called Alena's number. He listened to it ring but didn't leave a message. Where was she? If she hadn't found an open door around the back, she should've come in the front. That made him wonder if she'd encountered the other man, Steve.

"Is he here?" Hank took a step toward Matthew. "Is your partner in this hangar?" Fear for Alena rolled through him.

The pilot hung up. "They're sending more cops."

"Good." He stared down at Matthew. "Start talking."

"Like Liz did?"

"She got first dibs on a deal." Hank figured this guy knew how it went. He'd likely been arrested before, considering the ease with which he was handling this.

"Because she was stupid enough to get caught." Matthew maintained that belligerent expression.

"And Carol?"

Matthew snorted.

"Did you stab her, or was that your friend Steve? Whatever his name is."

His lips twitched a fraction. "He's good at that stuff. Just like he's good at charming old ladies out of their valuables."

Hank didn't want to know what else Steve was good at.

Dax wandered the room, using his nose to assess the space carefully.

Hank said, "How about you? Your skill set

run more toward attempted murder and bullying women? Robbing an armored truck when you're the one who chose to put your ill-gotten gains in there, and kidnapping. Let me guess, you're the brains and he's the muscle." Not that this guy lacked strength. It was more that Hank wanted to goad him into saying something.

Maybe explaining why they'd used the armored truck to transport the stolen jewels in the first place. There had to have been easier ways to get the loot from the resort.

Unless there had been something specific on the truck they also took.

Matthew studied him. Probably trying to figure out how to play it.

A police car pulled into the hangar, blue and red lights flashing against the glass window and on the wall by the door, where Dax sniffed at the crack underneath.

"Whatcha got there, Dax?"

His dog kept sniffing.

Two cops came in. "Busy night, Miller."

"It's not over." Hank pointed to Matthew. "One for holding, one for the hospital." He turned to indicate the man who'd been held hostage. "One more suspect at large, but we don't have an ID, so we have no idea what he looks like."

Dax pawed at the spot under the door.

"Dax, come."

His dog barked.

"Guess he smells bacon through there." One of the officers chuckled.

"Take care of this, please." Hank needed to figure out what was going on with Dax. Especially because Alena hadn't come in here. He strode over. "Dax."

The K-9 sat immediately.

Hank tugged the door open and gasped. Dax ran between his legs and the door. Hank glanced back over his shoulder. "Get an ambulance."

Then he knelt beside where Alena lay, out cold. A knot on her forehead.

The door at the end of the hall was slightly cracked. Dax ran to it and sniffed at the outside air through the tiny gap. "Dax, come." He didn't want his dog running out into the night.

Whoever had done this could be hanging around outside.

"Alena." He touched her shoulder while sickness roiled in his stomach. "Alena, can you hear me?"

She gasped and started to sit up. "Chadwell."

SIXTEEN

Alena hauled open the door to the interview room, using the movement to shake off the raging headache. Using her good hand, because the other one was almost useless. She'd argued the EMT down to a bandage and would follow up with her doctor later. Alena was pretty sure it was a broken wrist, but if she kept it still and didn't use it, she would be okay. She had her gun back. She couldn't fire it without screaming in pain, but that was a bridge she would cross when she came to it.

There was a case to work.

"I'll come with you." His voice made her want to turn, step into his arms and stay there.

It made her want to soak up his warmth in a hug and let all the pain fade into the background. She'd had to settle for over-the-counter meds because she didn't want to waste hours waiting for the Emergency Department doctors to process her through.

She turned to Hank, wanting to say yes. So badly. But he knew why she couldn't let him take the weight of this. "Give me a minute." She added, "Please." Mostly because she was too achy to want to get into a longer discussion.

They'd pulled the arrest record for Chadwell and his FBI file had been sent over by ASAC Waterson. She'd had to explain to everyone in Hank's department that she'd been working a case two years ago and not realized until it was too late that her boyfriend was the prime suspect.

Her cheeks still burned from the embarrassment. Added to the pain of her injuries, Alena wanted to curl up on a couch and cry.

Right now, she needed a moment alone in a serious way, but she would have to settle for a few minutes with Elizabeth so she could pull together a shot at finding him and saving herself even more of the embarrassment of being duped so badly.

Hank's expression softened in a way she did *not* need right now. "I'll be right next door."

Chief Willa walked by, behind him. They were both going to listen in, apparently.

Alena stepped into the interview room and closed the door.

"I have nothing more to say to you." Elizabeth sniffed. "I'm thinking maybe I need a lawyer."

"That's certainly your prerogative." Alena laid the file folder on the table. "If you'd like."

"Whatever. Just ask what you wanna ask."

That gave Alena leave to sit, open the file and slide the photo across the table. "Have you ever seen this man before?"

Elizabeth leaned forward in her chair to stare at the photo. "Uh, *yeah*. That's Steve."

Alena's stomach flipped over. She ignored the need to run to the bathroom and took a long breath. "Earlier tonight, he knocked me out. He shoved my head against a wall so hard, I lost consciousness."

Elizabeth shrugged. "So?"

Alena studied the young woman. "He's done that to you before?"

"He's a guy." Elizabeth shrugged. "Guys get intense."

Alena couldn't imagine Hank, or his brother, or a lot of the men she knew, ever doing something like that. But Chadwell? That was a life she'd lived. Through the good and the bad. All the times where she'd been too naïve, through having to face her blindness and see the truth instead.

"His real name is Chadwell Jenkins."

Elizabeth frowned.

"Two years ago, he was my boyfriend. I was an FBI agent working a case. I didn't realize until too late that the prime suspect was him."

"So he pulled one over on you." Elizabeth's expression turned to a smirk. "Join the club."

"You participated in criminal activity."

"Under duress… Isn't that what it's called?" Elizabeth shifted in her chair and her chin rose. "Right?"

"That is right. I can't say I'm able to plead that defense. It is a good one." Alena needed to get this woman to sympathize with her. Or she just needed to get Elizabeth talking.

Hank had wanted to take some time to talk about how she felt about Chadwell being part of this. Alena had brushed off his concern for that, and her wrist.

Why drag it all back up? The important thing right now was finding him. The guy had all the jewels and all the money. So how did they locate him before he got away with a crime? Again.

"When I arrested him and brought him in, he ended up getting away on a technicality." Alena sat back in her chair. "You can guarantee I'm not going to let that happen again. But that means I need your help, Elizabeth. Guys like Chadwell and Matthew? It's not okay what they do. Chadwell needs to be in prison. For good this time."

Elizabeth just stared at her, but Alena could see her thinking it over.

Alena kept her injured arm on her stomach,

hoping it wasn't too obvious she was cradling it. She'd tugged the sweater sleeve over the bandage. "Who stabbed Carol?"

"That would've been Steve." She pointed to the photo. "Whatever his name is."

"Chadwell."

Elizabeth shrugged. "He's the one who stabbed her."

"And who kidnapped you?"

Elizabeth swallowed. "That was Matthew."

The veneer of her bravado had begun to crack. Alena could see the scared young woman in over her head underneath. "That must've been hard. What was it about?"

Elizabeth stared at the photo. The table. Anything but Alena. "Threatening Steve with killing me didn't work, so he pushed me off that hill. Tried to kill me. Or, at least, leave me for dead. I guess he didn't think that dog would find me so fast."

"He should have." Alena shifted without moving her arm. "Things like that landed him in jail."

Elizabeth blinked.

"The Sundown Valley Police Department arrested Matthew a short time ago." Around the same time she was getting into it with Chadwell. "He's done."

"Where are the jewels?"

"You tell me." It wasn't great that Elizabeth

knew the police and Alena had no idea where to find the haul, but they needed Chadwell in cuffs. "Leaving on a plane didn't work. Chadwell is in the wind. I can only assume he has the haul. All of it. Where would he go?"

"How am I supposed to know?"

"Maybe because you're the one who knows him better than anyone." Alena shrugged. "Maybe because I'm out of options on people to ask. He's in the wind, and if I don't save face with the Bureau, I get put on probation again. Because he pulled one over on me. Again. I'm not exactly in a forgiving mood. So the more you tell me, the easier it goes for you, and the worse it goes for Chadwell—or Steve. Do you really want to be the one behind bars while he's off on some beach?"

The bit about her possible probation wasn't precisely true, but regulation allowed her some leeway with the truth.

Elizabeth pressed her lips into a thin line, as if she bit down on them.

"If Carol dies, he's looking at murder charges. That's life in prison." Alena kept her tone steady. "So, where would he go? He doesn't know this local area. Did you meet up anywhere in town while you've been here? Is he staying some-where?"

Elizabeth stared at the table.

Alena would be her but for the grace of God in her life. She didn't know why one person walked one path while another walked something different. She was an FBI agent. As long as that was true, it was what she was going to be. "Tell me where I can find him."

Hank stared at her through the glass.

Elizabeth said, "There's a cabin on the resort property. They let people rent them, whole places like rentals not hotel rooms."

Alena said, "Which one?"

"Number eighteen. On the west side of the lake."

Chief Willa moved toward the door. "I'll get with the manager. Find out who at the resort is the weak link these guys used to get their stuff off the property and into that armored vehicle. And see if that person knows why they chose it."

The door closed behind him. Hank just kept staring at Alena. Since he'd found her in that hall, not knowing if she was dead or just unconscious, it felt like his heart had stopped. Like she was the kind of woman it would destroy him to see walk away.

His ex? By the time Hank had signed the divorce papers, he'd been glad to get rid of a woman who would treat him like that. Someone who didn't want to be married to him. Why try and make it work when she'd already checked out? Now that he'd met Alena and spent time with her, he thought maybe she was a different kind of woman.

One he shouldn't let walk away.

Alena got up, grabbed her file and headed for the door of the interview room.

Hank met her in the hallway. He knew she was embarrassed about having to explain her connection to the man they were chasing. He had a story of his own, so why would he think her any less for trusting the man she loved?

It was on the tip of his tongue to explain that when she said, "We should get over to the resort."

Hank nodded. "Right."

She wanted to keep her distance. He needed to respect that—in a way he knew Chadwell didn't. Hank wasn't prepared to be anything like her ex. A man who would hurt a woman.

They headed for the bullpen and the crate where Dax snoozed. As soon as Hank crouched, the dog opened his eyes. A second later, he was on his feet. Hank opened the crate door and Dax walked into his arms. Hank gave him a full rubdown. "Hey, Dax." He leashed his partner.

Chief Willa walked out of his office, his cell phone still to his ear. "Cabin eighteen is registered to Jeremiah Johnson. I'll call you when I have the manager on his way to let you in."

Alena nodded. "That was one of his aliases when we were chasing him last time."

Hank wanted to squeeze her shoulder but instead said, "Let's go."

They headed for his K-9 vehicle, and he loaded Dax in the back. The drive would be at least fifteen minutes, even with lights and sirens—which they would turn off when they got close so as not to alert their suspect. Thankfully, she didn't just grab her phone and start scrolling. He wanted to talk to her.

"Can I tell you something?"

Alena shifted in her seat. "About the case?"

"Actually, no." Hank gripped the wheel and kept his eyes on the road. "It's about when Evan and I served."

"Okay." Her voice sounded so small.

He wanted to tug her in for a hug but that wasn't practical in a moving vehicle. Alena was the kind of woman he wanted to support—because she should have someone in her life who did that. "It was near the end of our time there. Evan wasn't in my unit, but his rotated through the same base. It was the first time we'd been on the same soil in three years."

Hank let the memories wash back. "My guys and I were on a routine patrol. Saw the wife of a translator we knew walking in the market with her son. Both of them beaten and limping." He blew out a breath and shook his head. "We pulled over. Her husband had been killed a couple of weeks before. She had no protection. The chiefs in her village wanted her to return to their ways. Submit. Hand over her son for training camp. She refused."

Alena hissed out a breath.

"We radioed in, trying to find out if we could help her." Hank's stomach clenched. "Request denied."

"Why?"

"We don't get to ask why. We get to follow orders." He let out a breath of his own. "So I told her to come to the base. I told her what to say. I told her precisely when to be there, and I was at the gate waiting when she did. Before anyone knew what was happening, I had the paperwork all processed. But I hadn't signed it."

He saw her shift in her seat, but she said nothing.

The headlights of an oncoming car flashed across them. Hank said, "I realized I was about to get hauled into the Captain's office and then Evan was there. He told me to go. He signed the paperwork and forced the hands of the state department guy so she could stay and claim amnesty. She lives in Baltimore. Her son just got a full ride to Harvard."

"Wow."

"Evan was court-martialed. Other-than-honorably discharged."

"No one knew it was you?"

Hank shook his head. "Evan was out walking with Fritz. That was my dog back then. Everyone thought he was me and assumed Evan told the truth about what happened."

"You saved her life. And her son's."

"But we can't save everyone." Hank had come to terms with that. "I did the little I could, but it doesn't stem the tide of evil in the world."

"So why tell me, if you feel like you didn't succeed?"

Hank pulled into the resort lot and parked. "Because I want you to know that I tried. That I did what I could because I'm the man I am, which is nothing like Chadwell."

"You think I don't know that?" Alena paused. "If things were different, of course I would…" Her voice trailed off. "Of course."

"So let's make things different." Hank leaned over the center console.

Hopefully Dax had gone back to sleep.

He stopped, one arm resting against the side of Alena's seat. Not crowding her but definitely in her space in a way she wasn't going to mistake. Then he let her make the next move. "Why not see what could be?"

Alena lifted her good hand. Her warm fingers

touched his face. "Why do I feel like that's the riskiest step I've ever taken?"

"Because you know how good it could be, and that's scary."

He heard her chuckle. "Hank…"

"I like the sound of that." Hank shifted a fraction closer, her fingers still on his face. Alena met him the rest of the way.

She touched her lips to his. Gentle at first, then she became more sure. Hank wanted to whoop but saved that for later—maybe when she wasn't watching. He tilted his head and leaned into the kiss, wondering where things might go.

It didn't have to be heavy, and he wasn't asking for a lifetime commitment.

Yet.

Alena was the one he wanted to throw away all his good intentions for. She would be worth it, if they could figure out how to succeed at whatever this turned out to be.

This was a woman he could fall in love with.

Dax's hot breath washed over the side of his face. Hank pulled back and made a face. "Bro."

Alena chuckled. "I guess we know how he feels about that."

Hank's phone started to ring. Chief Willa's name popped up.

He shoved open the car door. "Time to end this."

SEVENTEEN

The resort manager stepped back from the door to cabin eighteen, a master key card in his hand that he'd used to let them in.

Alena nodded. "Thanks."

At least he didn't try to go in ahead of them. That would contaminate whatever evidence they might find inside. And, for all they knew, Chadwell could be hiding in there, unaware they were about to enter.

"Housekeeping told me the occupant refused them entry. He told them not to come in at all."

She nodded again. From where she stood on the tiny porch of the cabin beside the lake, she could see the freshly cleared paths that crisscrossed the area around the resort. More snow had fallen overnight, but they'd ensured residents could move around the property and explore still. In fact, it looked beautiful with the freshly fallen snow—even if the dump of winter precipitation meant the roads in and out of town and the airport were closed.

Too bad enjoying the scenery wasn't why she was there.

Hank let Dax off his leash and cracked the door wide enough for him to squeeze through. "He'll flush out anyone inside."

Alena waited on the porch, gun drawn. Between the fact Chadwell was here and that dizzying kiss Hank had given her in the car a few minutes ago, she couldn't grasp a single thought. Too many rolled through her mind, one after the other, threatening her focus.

She might be a professional, but she was also a human being.

A woman who'd had her heart broken.

With the storm, she had no backup except Hank and his department. Alena wasn't worried about being left unprotected.

Dax came back to the door.

Hank pushed it open. "There's no one inside."

He stepped in. Alena glanced back at the manager and caught an off expression on his face. She said, "Thanks," again so he'd know she didn't need him to come inside, then entered and shut the door behind her. Whatever that look was, she would figure out what it meant when they were wrapping up this case.

After they found her ex and arrested him.

Someone at the resort had betrayed their employer and committed a crime. Maybe the manager had an inkling of who it was—or he was trying to figure out how to spin this and keep from going to jail himself. Chadwell was the priority, since Carol was currently in the hospital fighting for her life, and a security guard at the resort had been beaten when the footage was deleted.

Seemed like Chadwell was trying to cover his tracks.

"Is he a clean-living-space type of guy?"

Hank's question jogged her out of her thoughts. Alena glanced at him, trying to think and not be distracted by the fact this good man—this cop—was everything she'd ever wanted. A guy she could trust and count on. He wouldn't ever betray her, or force her to risk the oath she'd taken to uphold the law.

And that kiss?

Alena warmed just thinking about it.

She had to answer his question. Alena cleared her throat. "I don't think so." She shrugged. "Normal stuff like leaving shoes around, I guess. Waiting to do dishes until he *had* to." She looked around and saw why he asked. "This place is clean. Too clean."

"That's what I was thinking."

She walked through the kitchen area, where

there was nothing in the sink. The dishwasher was empty. Minimal food in the fridge like condiments the previous person never finished so they hadn't thrown away the bottle. "It looks like I'd expect it to if I had just arrived to stay."

He circled the living room. Dax had settled down by the front door, where he stared at her. She watched Hank for a second because Dax had already cleared the rest of the cabin. Alena let out a long sigh.

She couldn't help thinking she'd been swept away by Chadwell, and he'd broken her heart.

There was nothing to indicate Hank would or wouldn't do the same thing, except she was far more inclined to trust this man. He was precisely the kind of guy her father would love for her to fall for.

Alena gave the bathroom and one bedroom a cursory look. "Where is he?"

Chadwell had to be the focus, but he wasn't there.

Hank stood at the bedroom door. He might be trustworthy, but he'd shared his darkest secret with her. Had she done the same? No. That meant in this relationship—or whatever they had going on—*she* was Chadwell.

"I need to tell you something."

Hank frowned. "About your ex?" The look on his face actually made her feel better. Unlike everyone she worked with, who only saw her failure, Hank seemed to be angry with Chadwell.

But she couldn't think about that right now. Not when, with everything, he seemed to get a little bit more perfect. There was still something hanging in the air between them. She didn't want to get into this with finding Chadwell so deep that they didn't have the chance for her to be completely honest.

Alena pushed out a long breath. "My father had a stroke four months ago."

Hank shifted slightly, almost a flinch. "A stroke."

"He's got a nurse now, and he's in therapy to help him get his speech back. He has to relearn a lot of things." Alena took a quick breath so she could force the rest of it out. "I've been writing his newsletter for him."

Hank nodded. "I thought the tone had changed."

"I just…" She looked at the floor for a second. "I didn't want an untruth between us, even if it isn't serious and doesn't have anything to do with the case. It's important to both of us."

Hank crossed the room. He wrapped his arms around her in a quick hug. "Thank you."

Her cheeks warmed. "You're welcome."

Alena didn't know what else to do, so she slid back the closet door. "Whoa."

Two black duffel bags lay on the carpeted

floor. Stuffed with contents, by the looks of them. She used her sweater sleeve to pull back the zipper that had a cutout on the tag part, making it impossible to pull prints from anyway. Just so she could see inside.

She did the same with the other duffel.

"I'm thinking if we pull all this out, it's going to turn out to be every jewel switched with a fake from every person at this medical conference."

"I think you're probably right."

"So why did he leave it?" Alena peered into the duffel. One of them had a cell phone close to the top. She frowned and used her sleeve to remove it.

"Here." He waved his gloved hand. She'd left her winter gloves in the car, so she handed him the phone. Hank held it so he didn't smudge too many existing prints but there wasn't much they could do when time was a factor. They couldn't wait days for print identification to come back. "Doesn't have a passcode."

She frowned. Who didn't put that basic protection on their phone? "Same as Elizabeth with her tablet and the GPS."

Hank grunted, all his attention on the phone screen.

"What is it?"

"No calls or texts. One photo in the gallery,

and other than that, it's been wiped. Or it was only used for this one thing." Hank turned the phone so she could see the screen.

Chadwell stared back. A bathroom mirror selfie where he held the stolen million-dollar necklace in one hand and the phone in the other. Across the bottom he'd added text.

Try harder next time.

Hank's heart wanted to break for her, and the look on Alena's face. More than just being embarrassed, he could see that every action of Chadwell's was another twist of the knife he'd stabbed in her back—figuratively, of course. Hank was going to make sure it didn't happen literally.

Chief Willa had emailed to say Matthew wasn't talking. They were still trying to pin down his real identity from his prints and a DNA swab. Until then, there wasn't much they could do but hold him and wait for the local county prosecutor to return to the office on Monday morning.

Hank wanted Chadwell in cuffs before then. "We have the jewels now, at least. People can get their property back after it's processed as evidence."

Alena nodded. "He only needed the necklace.

He can sell that and disappear with the proceeds. And it's a whole lot more portable and easier to get away with—than two duffel bags."

"And he wanted to leave you a parting gift."

Alena pressed her lips together and said nothing.

"Just because Chadwell is a jerk who purposely wants to make life miserable for you, doesn't mean you aren't a good agent."

Alena rolled her eyes. "It shouldn't, but of course that doesn't prevent me from feeling like maybe it does."

"Are you going to let him get away?"

"Of course not."

"Good." Hank nodded. "So let's go find him."

After that kiss and her sharing what she'd been holding back, he couldn't help thinking they'd turned a corner in this. She had told him the truth about her father's condition. How she'd been managing things through his recovery, in what had to be a scary time she'd faced alone. Even though Alena hadn't gone into thorough detail about all the things she'd had to face and how scared she'd been, he could figure it out.

Hank wanted to help her sort this thing with Chadwell so she could let go of at least part of what she'd been carrying.

Still, that left them with a long-distance relationship at best. It left them with one of them having to uproot their life and give up their career in order for it to work.

Hank sighed. At least this case could be over for her. After that, they could figure out if there was anything to their relationship past this weekend. It was time to find Chadwell.

Hank took the phone to Dax, praying that his dog would be able to find a scent on the mobile device. He called out before he even reached the living area, where Dax waited. So, when he came into view, the dog was already shaking off the static of waiting and ready to work.

"Wanna go, Dax? Wanna get it?"

The dog shifted on his feet, ears lifted.

"Get it." Hank held out the phone.

Dax sniffed all around it. If he couldn't get a good scent, he would indicate as such. But after a few seconds' inhaling, he sat.

"Good boy." Hank clipped on his leash. "He'll probably circle the cabin a few times before we go outside, so hang here."

Alena nodded. Hank said, "Dax, seek!"

The dog did move through the cabin a few times. Hank heard Alena on the phone, calling in officers to guard the jewels in case they were about to leave. Dax spent time sniffing the duffel bags. The tiny trash can in the bathroom and the edge of the counter. He ignored the bed, which told Hank that Chadwell hadn't slept here even if Elizabeth had met him here.

Alena was standing with the manager when Hank and Dax came outside. Two uniformed officers headed their way. She told Bremerton, "You stay out here," and called to the officers, "Duffel bags in the bedroom closet!"

Then she turned to Hank.

Dax sniffed around the packed-down snow. He would find the freshest scent and follow that, hopefully leading them to where Chadwell had hidden. The spot he planned to stay at until the storm cleared enough he could escape town.

The last thing Hank wanted was to be forced to stand down because Chadwell had made it all the way to someone else's jurisdiction. He wanted to find this guy—and soon.

Hank followed his dog, giving Dax the freedom to do his job. The K-9 wound on the path around to the back side of the cabin, which faced the lake. He checked and saw Alena following. "You don't have your gloves and we don't know how long this is going to take."

Alena stuck her hands in her pockets. "I'm good." She kept a steady pace, sticking with him and Dax.

Hank figured having her at his back wasn't a bad thing. He could keep an eye on her and they were each as motivated as the other to find Chadwell.

Though, he didn't think she wanted it for the same reason he did—for this to be over for her.

Dax followed the scent along a path that had been dug out by an ATV with a plow attachment, judging by the sides and the ground under his feet, which was just packed-down snow. It circled the lake and headed into the trees.

"You think he hiked all the way out of town?" Alena asked.

Hank thought about this area. "There are cabins dotted around in the woods that spread out from the resort. We'll be over the property line pretty quickly, but the state parks department keeps it maintained because they rent cabins all year round. Even in snow like this. There are spots that are gorgeous, especially because of the snow, where you leave your car in a parking lot by the highway and hike all your gear in with you. Spend the weekend snowed in by a fire."

"I'm so tired that having no electricity and no WiFi sounds amazing."

Hank chuckled. "More of a hotel girl?"

"After this weekend? I'm thinking a beach. Even a hot cup of coffee would be good about now."

"I'll make sure you have one, first chance we get." He also wanted to take her to dinner, but until Chadwell was in cuffs, that wasn't going to happen.

Dax led them over a mile down a thin trail toward a tiny cabin. Probably all one room, with a basic kitchen hooked up to the gas tank beside the structure. No electricity. No shower. The kind of place that felt like camping but had wood walls, not the canvas of a tent.

"This time you take the back door."

Hank smiled. After what had happened at the hangar, he didn't blame her. She had injuries but refused to allow them to slow her down, whether out of determination or sheer stubbornness. Being raised by a marine corps general, he figured it was likely both.

He headed around for a rear exit as the cabin would have two points of entry and exit, even if the back was only a window. He could break glass if necessary.

Dax shifted, alerting in a tiny way.

Unsure what he had noticed with those canine senses and his training, Hank turned, his gun already out.

The manager from the resort had followed them, and he had a gun. He lifted it, aiming to fire at Hank's chest. Finger on the trigger. That look in Bremerton's eyes Hank had learned to spot before it meant it was too late for him.

Bremerton fired.

EIGHTEEN

Alena turned in the tiny cabin she'd been look-ing around, not wanting to stay long when it smelled faintly like natural gas. She stared at the open door. "Gunshot."

She raced to the door and jumped off the porch first. Alena ran toward the sound, her heart pounding at what she might find.

Dax barked.

Snow sprayed up and she spotted two men roll. Tangled together, Hank fought with the re-sort manager. Battling for a grip on his gun.

Alena spread her feet to stabilize her balance and yelled, "FBI! Drop the weapon or I will shoot you."

Hank didn't quit. The manager could take ad-vantage of it if he did. She watched Bremerton realize there was no point arguing with them. He had to know trying to use that gun would get him killed. Alena recognized the moment he understood there was no point struggling.

It was over.

Hank took the manager's gun. He backed up, sitting back on his heels. Sweat on his hairline. Breaths coming fast. "Roll over. Hands behind your back."

The manager stared at him.

"Now."

With a huff, the man did as asked. Alena kept her gun aimed at him, just in case. *Where was Chadwell?* "There's no one inside. Chadwell isn't here."

"You think Dax got it wrong?" Hank's brows rose.

"Well, maybe not..."

"Chadwell was here," Hank said. "Otherwise Dax wouldn't have brought us."

"Unless it was this guy's scent he caught from that phone." Alena waved at the resort manager, now on his front.

Hank cuffed him, then had Bremerton sit on the edge of the porch. Dax leaned froward and growled. Instead of questioning him, Hank glanced at Alena. "Wanna take another look inside?"

Alena shook her head. "There's no one in there. No evidence. No Chadwell."

Hank turned back to the manager. "Where is he?"

The guy made a face and glanced aside.

"Great. We'll assume you're the one behind this instead then, and you can take the fall for it all. Cheating your guests. Attempted murder. The attack on your security guard." Hank folded his arms. "Is that what's going to happen here?"

"I didn't do all that!"

"But you did plenty." Alena figured he'd at least been leaned on to get involved—or paid off to. But her gut said Chadwell was definitely here. Where else would this guy have obtained a photo of her ex? "So start talking and maybe you can save yourself from life in prison."

Bremerton's expression shifted. He knew he had no leverage. He'd been found out. "I'm not a thief."

"But you helped them." Alena wanted to shake him and ask where Chadwell was. Her heart didn't even care about this guy—but her professionalism had to override what she wanted. Otherwise, she would be back to that woman who'd been duped in the first place.

She needed to be better now. Less naïve, smarter and more in control of her emotions. Chadwell was here. She was going to find him and arrest him. She would make sure all the evidence and procedure followed exact protocols or he would only end up being released on a technicality again.

She wasn't going to let that happen.

Not when God, in His grace, had given her a second chance. A way to make up for who she had been, set everything to rights and make sure justice was finally served. This was her chance to finally put her past to rest. Maybe even move toward the future.

Capturing Chadwell was the way to do that.

"I didn't have a choice." He still didn't look at them.

Hank said, "They paid you?"

"Not yet."

She wondered if the manager was mad he'd been strung along and cut out at the last minute. Maybe he'd been there at the lakeside cabin because he'd wanted the money he'd been promised. He might be as motivated to find Chadwell as they were.

Alena said, "Did you have a meeting spot? A place to go after this was all over?"

Bremerton shook his head.

"What about a phone number, or another way to contact them?" Alena set her hand on her hip. If their suspect had been here earlier but wasn't here now, they were one step behind him. Or more than that.

"It's an app. But I'm not giving you access to my cell phone without a warrant." He lifted his chin. "I know my rights, and you only have hearsay that I'm involved."

Hank said, "That and the fact you just tried to murder me. Good thing for me, you missed."

Alena sucked in a breath. Hank could have died.

She wasn't sure why it hit her just then. She'd heard that gunshot. But for some reason the thought of being alone out here with him bleeding out and no chance for emergency services to arrive in time made her heart squeeze in her chest. For a second, she didn't even think about Chadwell.

Dax leaned against her leg in a moment of solidarity. As if he knew, in his dog way, that she needed comfort.

Alena ran her cold fingers over his head, wincing when pain lanced through her wrist.

Hank said, "This is your shot to try to fix what you've done. Get yourself in good standing with the police—" he motioned to himself then her "—and the FBI. Maybe save yourself unnecessary grief."

The resort manager shivered. He still wore his wool overcoat, but those shoes he had on with the suit and tie weren't conducive to being outdoors. They'd need to make sure he didn't get hypothermia.

Finally, he said, "I knew he was using this place, so I followed you."

Alena needed to know where Chadwell was

now. "Did he get here from the resort? Or another way?" She wanted to know if he had a car.

"The road." The manager motioned with his chin since his hands were cuffed behind his back. "He has a car parked up there."

That, if he'd used it, meant the vehicle was gone, along with her ex.

"Let's go." Alena grasped his arm. "Back to the resort." Where the officers from Hank's department could arrest him and take him to jail.

A shudder moved through Bremerton's body. She could feel his tension.

She tugged him to start walking. He pulled his arm from her grasp and rushed up the steps into the cabin. Dax raced after him. The manager kicked the door shut and the dog slammed into it.

Alena tried the door handle. "He locked it."

That would have taken some twisting, and he'd done it fast. But the door was locked now. Hank nudged her aside. "Let me."

"What is he doing?" Alena stepped out of the way.

"Nothing good."

She moved to the window and tried to peer between the blinds while Hank kicked at the door. He let out a grunt of frustration. She spotted the resort manager in the kitchen. "He's doing something at the stove." She frowned.

"He can't be trying to melt off the cuffs. That won't—"

With his back to the drawer, Bremerton grabbed a flame lighter.

"He's going to—"

Hank kicked the door open.

"No!" Before the resort manager lit the gas. Before Hank ran inside, Alena rushed past Dax, shoving him out of the way. She slammed into Hank and knocked him off the porch. *That smell of gas.*

The cabin exploded.

"Hank!"

Hank's back hit the snow. A fireball erupted above him, beyond where Alena lay stretched out on him. She'd saved his life. "Hey." He patted her shoulder.

Alena didn't move.

He rolled her to the snow beside him. Alena's head flopped to the side, her eyes closed.

Hank shifted to her. "Alena." He patted her cheek. "Alena, wake up."

She didn't move. He pressed two fingers to her throat and felt a faint pulse. "Alena."

Tears filled his eyes. *I would give anything.* He just wanted her to wake up. Smile at him. He wanted her to be all right. Able to see her ex put in prison—to know she'd closed the case. That they had done it together.

God, help—

Alena gasped. Her eyes flew open.

Hank scrambled closer so she woke up to him, not the overwhelming fear he'd faced. The idea that he might lose her forever.

"Hey."

She blinked. Her hand shifted by her side and grasped his elbow.

"Dax!" Hank also needed to know the dog was all right. When he trotted into view and licked Hank's face, such relief rolled through him that he allowed it for a second even though it was gross. "All right. Thanks for that, Dax."

Hank nudged Dax back and sat up. "Alena, are you okay?"

She pushed out a breath and sat up also. "He blew himself up." Tears filled her eyes.

Hank tended to take a more pragmatic approach. "He didn't want to live with the embarrassment and the consequences of his actions." Maybe that made him sound heartless, but for a cop who saw stuff like this regularly, it helped to keep his emotions healthy rather than descend into depression and grief over a life ended too quickly.

Alena nodded. "He knew exactly what he was doing."

"And he made this choice. Nearly killing us in the process." Hank didn't like that part. The manager could have killed Dax the same way he could've killed Hank or Alena. Three cops who didn't deserve to get swept up in his taking his life, yet they would've been more collateral damage for the choices Bremerton had made.

Hank held his hand out for Alena and helped her stand. She stepped into his arms. To his surprise, she said, "Thanks."

Hank frowned. "You're the one who saved my life. And Dax's. That was quick thinking."

As it was, the door had blown off the cabin. The roof had collapsed in and there was a decent blaze going—and would be until they could get the gas turned off. Heat from the fire took the edge off the cold, snowy afternoon.

Alena looked up at him, still in his arms.

"We should call in first responders and then get going." There was work to do, and staring at her like that made him want to pack it in. Pass responsibility to the rest of the department to find Chadwell while he took Alena to the hospital—and then out for something to eat.

There was a fantastic hole-in-the-wall burger place in town with the best fry sauce in the state.

Hank leaned down and kissed her quicker than he wanted to. Then he made a call. As soon as he hung up, he said, "Come on."

He stepped back and took her hand. They walked together to the resort with Dax behind them. More trudging through snow. A little shell-shocked. More than a few bumps and bruises. Alena was doing great pushing through the pain in her wrist even with the bandage and medicine.

He took a deep breath and pain echoed through his ribs from being tackled off the porch. She'd saved his life, but he'd probably still get an X-ray. He wanted to ask her if she'd ever consider moving to Montana. Maybe she wasn't prepared to give up her career and he'd have to consider leaving this town. Find a police department somewhere else.

Hank sighed.

She glanced over but said nothing.

Instead, the quiet hung between them around the lake back to the cabin where the jewels had been found. Two officers stood at the door, chatting. Drinking coffee from paper cups. "Everything good?" Hank asked them.

They both nodded. He explained what had happened with the resort manager and asked them to recover Bremerton's body.

One of the officers grabbed his radio. "On it."

Hank nodded. His phone rang, tucked deep in his pants pocket under the hem of his jacket and the sweater he'd pulled over his vest. When he dug it out, he glanced at Alena. "It's Evan." His brother was watching Elizabeth's dog. Was that why he was calling? Hank swiped the screen. "What's up, Ev?"

Alena paced away a couple of steps. Thinking through their next move? He should be doing that, too.

Evan said, "Someone is outside creeping around." He paused. "They just crashed over one of the trash cans."

"And the dog?"

"With me. Barking, but I shushed her and picked her up. I think someone is breaking in."

"Then call 9-1-1." He was working. His brother should know better than to bother him when he was working, and Evan could get officers to respond if he genuinely needed help. "It's probably—"

"It's that guy you're looking for."

"Chadwell?" The second he said that, Alena spun around. Hank started walking toward the car and she jogged with him. "How do you know?"

"I was at the police station after you. I saw a picture on the board." Evan paused. "He just walked by the back window. He's coming in."

"Hide, Ev. Don't risk yourself. Please." Hank ran faster, Dax beside him. He'd faced losing Alena today. He didn't want to go through the same with his brother. He got the dog loaded up in record time and climbed in the front seat, Alena already buckled beside him. "I'm gonna lose you for a second while the car connects."

"Just get here."

When the car Bluetooth connected, he realized his brother had hung up. Hank flipped on lights and sirens and called for a unit to meet him at his brother's, in case officers on patrol could get there faster.

It seemed like an eternity to get across town, but was probably more like ten minutes with the speed he drove. He prayed they wouldn't hit ice, and that prayer was answered.

He skidded the vehicle to a stop outside Evan's house. Alena raced for the house and he got Dax out quick, not even taking time to leash him up. Alena kicked the front door right beside the lock. She got it partway open. Hank finished it for her, and Dax raced in.

He knew Evan's house, so the dog would know who to look for. His read on their actions told him something was wrong. Dax was a smart dog.

They heard a bark and growl from deep in the house. Hank ran for Evan's bedroom, the bathroom through the closet. Good place to hide.

A gunshot rang out.

"Dax!"

He could hear Alena right behind him. Then a high-pitched bark from inside the bathroom. A crash, and glass shattered. Dax barked, low and mean. He was mad—but as long as he hadn't been shot, Hank would be able to breathe.

He crossed the threshold, gun first. Evan sank to the floor, blood running down his face.

Chadwell stood in the middle of the room, holding Elizabeth's dog by the scruff of its neck while the Chihuahua wriggled her legs. Dax lifted his front paws off the ground and barked at Chadwell, the sound muffled because he had something in his mouth.

Hank aimed his gun. "Drop the gun and set the dog—" glass covered the tiled floor "—in the bathtub."

Chadwell swung his gun around. Hank didn't have a clear shot because of the tiny dog.

Alena moved beside him, her gun also pointed at her ex. "Gun down. You're under arrest."

Chadwell winced. "Okay. Okay." A man who didn't want to get shot. He crouched and set his gun down.

"Dax, out." Hank didn't want his dog to get cuts on his feet. And he should figure out what Dax had in his mouth. "Loose." Dax spat what looked like the Chihuahua's collar on the floor.

"What…?" Hank frowned.

Dax picked it up again.

Chadwell dropped the little dog into the tub, where it yapped and pranced around, then put two paws on the side of the bath and barked again. Defiance flashed in the man's eyes.

Alena said, "See to Evan. I've got this."

Hank kept his gun handy and crouched beside his brother while Alena had Chadwell turn around. He heard the satisfying clink of cuffs being secured and listened to her read him his Miranda rights. Hank called for an ambulance for his brother, who had a steady and strong pulse despite the blood and the fact he'd been knocked out.

It was done. The case was over. Alena looked over, Chadwell facing the shower door, and grinned.

Hank couldn't bring himself to grin back.

She was leaving.

NINETEEN

"Yes, sir." Alena gripped the phone, standing in almost the same spot as when she'd talked to her dad and his nurse earlier today. She could hardly believe this was actually over. Case closed. Exhaustion weighed on her like a bomb squad suit.

She paced the police station hallway to keep blood flowing so she didn't fall asleep on her feet and said, "We have Chadwell in custody. We caught him breaking and entering, we've got him on assault. We're working on the other charges."

Like finding out why he would ever risk his freedom just to get to Elizabeth's dog. It didn't make sense. But that was why Hank and Chief Willa were currently talking to her. So they could find out.

Alena had no interest in talking to Chadwell long enough to say hi, let alone ask why he'd done all this. Matthew wasn't talking. Carol was stable, but hadn't regained consciousness. The resort manager had taken his own life. Evan was currently at the hospital and they were waiting for word on his condition.

"Good," ASAC Waterson said through the phone. "I'll contact the marshals for extradition back to Wyoming. You stay there and talk to the judge. Get the paperwork sorted, and I'll see you here when you're back. The Allentown case is heating up."

"Yes, sir."

He hung up.

Alena slumped against the wall. Hardly able to believe she'd actually arrested Chadwell— again. Hopefully this time the charges would stick. She was going to ensure she did everything right so there was no room for his lawyer to again come up with some technicality that would get him off free. He would face multiple charges across two states. No way would he get away with this.

The interview room door opened. Hank stepped out first, followed by Chief Willa. Hank said, "The dog's collar." He walked past her into the bullpen.

Alena waited for the chief, not liking the awkwardness that seemed to have developed between them now the case was over and the bad guy was in custody. "Chief?"

Willa said, "Apparently there's a miniature SD card with a GPS tracker on the dog's collar that Elizabeth had with all the designs for the fake jewels Chadwell makes. He's the forger."

She nodded. He had those skills, and he'd done it before. She just hadn't been able to get a conviction.

"It's evidence he's involved in this entire scheme, so he wanted to take it with him when he left town."

"What about the necklace he stole from that woman?"

Willa nodded. "Right. That was found on him when he was booked into holding. Taped to his abdomen."

Alena said, "I'm glad we recovered everything stolen."

"Let's go see if Hank has that flash drive."

She frowned but followed to the bullpen and saw Hank crouched in front of the dog crate by his desk. "No, Dax. Go back to sleep." Hank closed the door and stood, grinning. "He didn't want to give it up. Probably smells nice to him." He shifted the collar in his hands.

"Here we go." Hank tugged out a flash drive, barely bigger than the chip that had to be inserted in the computer port and no thicker. Just enough to hold and insert the drive. "Let's take a look."

He sat at his desk.

Alena found a seat across the aisle and sat so she could see his computer monitor. Her wrist screamed at her despite the pain meds she'd taken and the bandage the EMT had wrapped around it.

"You need to go get that checked out."

She lifted her face to Chief Willa. "You're probably right." She didn't want to know if it was broken or not. No matter how it felt, she would deal. Except she didn't have a ride to the hospital, so she'd have to get on the app and find a rideshare to pick her up. She also needed her things from Hank's house.

"Looks like what Elizabeth said. Drawings. Mockups of the jewelry with dimensions. His signature is at the bottom." Hank spun his chair around. "And more that we'll need to go through."

"I'll get the sergeant on it, if you'll submit that into evidence, Officer Miller."

Hank nodded.

"Soon as you're done, make sure Special Agent Sanchez sees a doctor. You probably want to go check on your brother, so take her with you."

Hank didn't look at her. "Yes, sir."

She drank a cup of coffee, writing out her report, while he finished up his. Hank walked her out to his car and drove her to the hospital. She didn't know what to say to this man she respected a whole lot, who she absolutely cared for, and might also be falling for.

If she wasn't already in love with him.

But what was the point of even acknowledging that when all it would do was remind her how much of her life would have to change? If she admitted she loved Hank, then she'd also have to admit she'd been looking for a change. Was she going to be a woman who gave up her whole career for a man?

If she turned that around the other way, she'd have to ask what there was for her with the FBI that was worth more than the happiness she could have with a good man like Hank. Not that he'd said he loved her or anything like that. He cared. Was that enough to quit the FBI, and to move herself and her father to Montana?

Hank pulled up to the front door. "You go in. I'll check on my brother and come find you." Still, he pulled up the parking brake and came around.

She reached for the door handle with her injured arm and realized why he'd gotten out. Hank opened the door for her. Alena unlatched her seat belt, which took more effort for her exhausted body than it should. He held her other arm as she climbed out.

Alena couldn't resist. She lifted up on her toes and kissed him. "Thank you."

She heard his intake of breath. His arms wrapped around her and he kissed her back. Only when someone honked their horn did he pull back, and Alena rushed inside with her face flaming.

What was she going to do about Hank?

Hank wanted to go back to Alena first. Talk about that kiss. Instead, he left her to be treated—and probably have her wrist x-rayed—before she would likely be told to follow up with her doctor about a cast when the swelling had gone down. Her doctor in Wyoming. Hundreds of miles from here, in another state.

She would leave.

He didn't know what to say to make her stay, especially when that would mean her leaving her father.

Hank flashed his badge. The receptionist pointed him to a bay where Evan was being treated. He whipped back the curtain, taking out some of his frustration on how things were turning out with Alena, only to find Evan nose to nose with a nurse.

She looked mad, but his brother looked amused. And like he was enjoying himself. The nurse, a blonde a little younger than Evan, said, "Hold still."

Evan smiled. "This is more fun."

Hank grinned. He cleared his throat. "Sorry to interrupt."

"Are you here to arrest him?" the nurse said. "Wouldn't surprise me. He seems like the criminal type."

"Sadly, no." Hank laughed. "He's gonna live, right? I need someone to keep watching the Chihuahua."

Evan's expression glared daggers at Hank.

He just grinned at his brother, whose shirtless chest was covered in bandages. The nurse taped another on Evan's forehead. "I think we're about done here."

Evan said, "Don't count on it."

She ignored him. "I'll probably be busy later. If you need anything, I'm sure the nurse that's mean to everyone, even little kids, can help you." She gathered all the trash and took her things with her, swiping the curtain closed on the way out.

Hank waited a second then said, "I don't know whether to commiserate with you, or go shake her hand."

Evan settled back in the bed and closed his eyes. "I'll see her again."

"And get arrested for stalking?"

"Trust me. It'll be fine."

Hank moved to the side of the bed. "Are you really okay? There was a lot of blood."

Evan opened one eye. "Worried about me?"

Hank didn't bother answering that. "How many stitches?"

"Only forty-seven."

Hank pushed out a breath. "Stay with me until you're healed."

"Because you feel guilty?"

"You keep getting hurt because of me." He counted Evan's dishonorable discharge in that. "Taking the fall. Getting hit with the fallout. You name it."

"The bad things that happen in my life aren't on you."

"Still."

"Uh, no." Evan shook his head. "I live my own life. I make my own choices. I let God lead me, and He takes care of it all. If I'm here, it's because He had a hand in keeping me alive when Chadwell came in. Besides, I'm your brother. Who else is going to face down a bad guy and save a Chihuahua for you?"

Hank pulled his brother up and gave him a hug.

Evan groaned. "Ow."

"Sorry." He let his brother lie back down.

"So what are you going to do about that girl?"

"You mean Alena?" Hank settled on the side of the bed.

"Who else would I mean?"

"What is there to do about her?"

Evan hit the side of Hank's arm with the back of his hand. "Are you going to answer all of my questions with questions for the rest of this conversation?"

Hank sighed. "I don't know what to do. She's leaving." Things between them…he didn't want to give that up. Not if he could help it.

"So go with her."

"Leave town?" He had family here. A life. But she could say that about Wyoming.

Evan said, "I'm gonna whack you again." He stared at Hank. "Is she worth giving up Dax for?"

Hank's stomach clenched. He didn't want to have to choose between them.

"Don't make promises to her you're never gonna keep. It's not fair to her." Evan shifted on the bed and winced. "But if you love her, then why let her walk away? It's not worth living another lonely day in your life. Make the sacrifice and get the girl. Maybe you can convince her of the merits of leaving the FBI and moving to Sundown Valley." He paused. "Summer might be good for that. She looked freezing."

Hank smiled. He looked at his shoes for a moment. Could he do it? The life he'd built here wasn't one it would be easy to give up. But for a strong woman with heart, a woman who knew what it felt like to fail the way he had. To face the consequences and keep going.

She was the kind of woman he wanted to build a future with.

However he could have that.

"I'll be back."

"Good." Evan closed his eyes. "I'm tired. Go tell her you love her and figure this out."

Hank squeezed his brother's shoulder. Why he'd taken the blame for what Hank had done... Well, if he was honest, he'd have done the same thing. He knew why Evan had done it. Hank wasn't going to let his brother suffer with the consequences any more than he already had. The way Alena shouldn't have to suffer the consequences of Chadwell's actions.

Justice would be served.

He flashed his badge again and was pointed in Alena's direction. He tugged the curtain back far enough to see inside, just in case he'd be disturbing her. Alena sat on the bed, her shoulders hitching, tears rolling down her face. Hank stepped in fast, then wondered if he was the reason she was crying.

He vacillated between staying and going. "I can..."

Alena let out a sob and covered her mouth with her hand.

Hank closed the distance between them and gathered her into his arms, settling on the bed so they were hip to hip. "Hey. Come here."

Alena sobbed against him, dampening his sweater with her tears. He rubbed a hand up and down her back. Prayed for her silently, and for himself, since it was probably about him as well as because she was exhausted, in pain, and it was finally over. Part relief. Part upset.

When she quieted down, he said, "Do you wanna talk about it?"

"No. It's embarrassing enough already." She stared at her phone on the bed.

"What happened?" Something might've happened with her father. Did she need to rush back home?

"Nothing." Alena shook her head. "It's dumb."

Hank didn't believe that for a second. "I know you're exhausted but you're also having real feelings."

"But I don't want to." She bit her lip.

"You don't want to what?" His stomach flipped over. Maybe he should leave.

Alena scrunched up her nose in a way that was completely adorable. "Be in love with you."

Ah. Hank didn't get any time to absorb that. Or to think about how he'd been feeling about her for a while now. Since before she tackled him off a porch and saved his life. "Is that such a terrible proposition?"

"It's not convenient to either of our lives. It'll make things weird. It doesn't help." Alena sighed. "It makes me not want to leave."

Hank touched her cheeks, rubbing tears away with his thumbs. "What if it was a good thing?"

"Shouldn't it be able to work?"

"You'd rather it was convenient and easy?"

Alena frowned.

"Or would you rather have the satisfaction of saying you fought for something that was worth fighting for and you won."

"Is that even possible?"

Hank said, "I think we should try. Because I'm in love with you, too." He touched his lips to hers. "And I wanna fight for us."

EPILOGUE

Six months later

Alena lifted the tray of coffee mugs, braced it with one hand and pushed open the screen door. Warm summer air hung on the back deck even though Hank and his brother had put up a shelter to shade the patio table and chairs from the weather.

She set the tray down and watched him, half-way down the long yard she hadn't seen that night she'd stayed in his guest room the weekend they'd met. Now she'd spent plenty of time out here.

Hank threw a ball, then another right after it, and two dogs ran down the yard.

Her father stood beside him, watching his German shepherd—a retired military working dog he'd adopted—run after a tennis ball alongside Dax.

Alena had quit the FBI two weeks after she'd

returned to Cheyenne. Sure, she'd wanted to move to Sundown Valley to be close to Hank, but there had been hurdles. Her career. Her father. When she'd mentioned everything to her dad, he'd insisted they come out here and look for a small cabin-style house. It was barely big enough for one person and a dog, let alone two people and her dad's new best friend. But with all the whispering between her dad and Hank, she'd figured it was best not to argue.

Going back to the office after she'd caught Chadwell should've been satisfying. Knowing she'd righted that wrong, and proven herself, was supposed to have made her feel good. Instead, it felt oddly like there was nothing left for her with the FBI.

She still got emails from her colleagues, mostly to razz her about her "demotion" to local police detective. As if. She loved investigating and being out in the community, getting to know people who lived there.

Her father had joined a local veterans group, and his dog accompanied him every time he went.

His social life was more active than hers. But, really, she just wanted to spend time with Hank.

The dogs started to play, ignoring the tennis balls now. Her dad and Hank turned to walk back to the porch. Her dad grabbed his coffee first and turned to watch the dogs while he drank. Hank pressed a kiss to her lips. "What was the call about?"

"Fingerprint result on the case with that missing teen."

Hank wound his arm around her waist. "Tell me where to search. Dax will find her."

Alena smiled. "Don't worry, I will as soon as we know where to look."

Hank gave her a squeeze then let go.

"Coffee first." Alena handed him his mug.

Hank grinned. "Always."

She leaned against him and watched the dogs play, tumbling and rolling across the sun-warmed grass.

"Well, that was a good cup of coffee." Her dad set the mug back on the tray, then yelled, "Titan, *hier*!"

His dog broke off from Dax and they both ran over, skidding to a stop. Titan sat beside her dad's leg and looked up at him. "We're gonna leave you kids to it." He gave Alena a kiss on the cheek and shook Hank's hand. "Have a good dinner."

Alena frowned. "Are we going somewhere?"

Hank's cheeks pinked. "Um…"

"Should I get changed?" She was wearing jeans and one of her nicer shirts, but had pulled a sweater over it instead of her good jacket. "I could swing by my house if we're going somewhere."

Dax barked.

Hank glanced over. "Come." He led his dog inside and crated him. "We can swing by your house on the way. You can do one of your quick changes, if you want, but you look just fine to me."

That was because he loved her—and he was a guy. Alena folded her arms. "Where are we going?"

Hank ran a hand down the Henley he had on. "Maybe I should change, too."

"Maybe you should spit out the answer to my question."

"We have reservations at Salvadore's."

Alena blinked. "At what time?" Salvadore's was an adorable restaurant she would *not* be wearing jeans to.

"Six."

"I only have an hour!" She raced for the door. "You'll have to pick me up. I'll need time to do my hair." She raced out the front door. As she backed her car off the drive, she saw Hank on his doorstep. Grinning.

He picked her up just before six, held her hand the whole way there. When he walked her into the restaurant, Hank in his tailored suit and Alena in the dark green dress she'd bought for a friend's wedding last year, the hostess brightened. "Wow, you guys."

She led them to a tiny table and Alena could feel people's attention on her. Finally for what she hoped was a good reason.

Hank held her chair.

"Everyone is staring."

He leaned down and kissed her. "Because you're beautiful."

Alena fingered the stem of her glass while he settled in his chair. He tugged her hand over and held her fingers in his. "Marry me."

Alena looked up. She hadn't wanted to hope. "I knew I wore the right earrings."

Hank laughed. "Marry me as soon as possible."

Alena couldn't help laughing with him. "Absolutely." There was nothing she wanted more for the future than to spend it with him.

He lifted her hand, slid a ring on her finger, and pressed a kiss there.

* * * * *

Dear Reader,

Each book I write is such an adventure and this one was no exception. I loved getting to know Alena and Hank, blending two worlds and two stories into one suspenseful tale. Each of us has things we wish we'd done differently in our lives, but God.

Those two little words "but God" mean so much to us as believers.

We were dead in our trespasses and sins, but God sent His son. We are swallowed up by pain and regret, but God lifts the weight from us and gives us peace and life. He gives us so much, there is truly no way we could say thank You enough for what He has done.

May God bless you as you read.

May He fill your life with gladness.

If you'd like to contact me, you can use the form on my website. Find it at www.authorlisaphillips.com, where you can sign up for my newsletter and receive a free book.

Happy Reading,
Lisa

Get 3 FREE REWARDS!

We'll send you 2 FREE Books <u>plus</u> a FREE Mystery Gift.

FREE Value Over **$20**

Both the **Love Inspired®** and **Love Inspired® Suspense** series feature compelling novels filled with inspirational romance, faith, forgiveness and hope.

YES! Please send me 2 FREE novels from the Love Inspired or Love Inspired Suspense series and my FREE gift (gift is worth about $10 retail). After receiving them, if I don't wish to receive any more books, I can return the shipping statement marked "cancel." If I don't cancel, I will receive 6 brand-new Love Inspired Larger-Print books or Love Inspired Suspense Larger-Print books every month and be billed just $6.49 each in the U.S. or $6.74 each in Canada. That is a savings of at least 16% off the cover price. It's quite a bargain! Shipping and handling is just 50¢ per book in the U.S. and $1.25 per book in Canada.* I understand that accepting the 2 free books and gift places me under no obligation to buy anything. I can always return a shipment and cancel at any time by calling the number below. The free books and gift are mine to keep no matter what I decide.

Choose one: ☐ **Love Inspired Larger-Print** (122/322 BPA GRPA) ☐ **Love Inspired Suspense Larger-Print** (107/307 BPA GRPA) ☐ **Or Try Both!** (122/322 & 107/307 BPA GRRP)

Name (please print)

Address   Apt. #

City   State/Province   Zip/Postal Code

Email: Please check this box ☐ if you would like to receive newsletters and promotional emails from Harlequin Enterprises ULC and its affiliates. You can unsubscribe anytime.

Mail to the **Harlequin Reader Service:**
IN U.S.A.: P.O. Box 1341, Buffalo, NY 14240-8531
IN CANADA: P.O. Box 603, Fort Erie, Ontario L2A 5X3

Want to try 2 free books from another series? Call 1-800-873-8635 or visit www.ReaderService.com.

---

*Terms and prices subject to change without notice. Prices do not include sales taxes, which will be charged (if applicable) based on your state or country of residence. Canadian residents will be charged applicable taxes. Offer not valid in Quebec. This offer is limited to one order per household. Books received may not be as shown. Not valid for current subscribers to the Love Inspired or Love Inspired Suspense series. All orders subject to approval. Credit or debit balances in a customer's account(s) may be offset by any other outstanding balance owed by or to the customer. Please allow 4 to 6 weeks for delivery. Offer available while quantities last.

Your Privacy—Your information is being collected by Harlequin Enterprises ULC, operating as Harlequin Reader Service. For a complete summary of the information we collect, how we use this information and to whom it is disclosed, please visit our privacy notice located at corporate.harlequin.com/privacy-notice. From time to time we may also exchange your personal information with reputable third parties. If you wish to opt out of this sharing of your personal information, please visit readerservice.com/consumerschoice or call 1-800-873-8635. **Notice to California Residents**—Under California law, you have specific rights to control and access your data. For more information on these rights and how to exercise them, visit corporate.harlequin.com/california-privacy.

LIRLIS23

LISCNM1223